I0690421

Modogamous

karen e. Martin

Cover Art: Sara E. Adrian
Cover Design: Cindy Patterson
Photography: Marquelle Garcia

Published November 30, 2013
by Two Signatures Productions

Copyright © 2013 Karen E. Martin

First Edition

All rights reserved. No part of this book shall be reproduced, stored in a retrieval system, or transmitted by any means— electronic, mechanical, photocopying, recording, or otherwise— without written permission from the publisher, except where permitted by law. All other registered trademarks or trademarks are property of their respective owners.

This is a work of fiction. Names, characters, places, and incidents either are products of the author's imagination or are used fictitiously. Any resemblance to actual events or locales or persons, living or dead, is entirely coincidental.

ISBN: 0-9844061-4-X
ISBN-13: 978-0-9844061-4-2

Dedicated to my amazing mother
and to my dear departed Dad
always in our hearts

CONTENTS

ACKNOWLEDGMENTS

No book would be complete without an acknowledgement of the people who have helped the author cross the publishing finish line. For *Modogamous*, those wonderful people include:

- Mom! For putting up with my late-night writing habits and morning grumpiness, and for being a truly inspirational woman in her own right.
- My two sisters, Beth and Mary, for being such a big help when I needed time to work on the book.
- My tireless sister-in-law, Crystal, who has really gone the extra mile to support me and to get the word out about my books. (You can visit Crystal's popular book blog at http://randommusesomy.blogspot.com/).
- The Chick Lit Goddesses (#GoddessLit on Twitter) and The Official Chick Lit Group (on Facebook), my online pals and author support system. I have learned so much from these ladies, who have cheered me on every step of the way, and made some real friends along the way.
- My wonderful beta readers, Liezl, Karen, and Melanie. Thank you, ladies, for your input, which helped so much in the writing of the book.
- The talented pair of artists who put together the beautiful cover of the book: Sara E. Adrian and Cindy Patterson.
- Ronni and Sian, two lovely ladies who helped me with some of the marketing legwork.
- All of my NaNoWriMo pals from 2012, who helped me keep plugging away at writing the book with endless word sprints and encouragement.
- Friends and fans who have continued to encourage me both online and in person. It has been a long road since I began writing this book more than a year ago, and your enthusiasm and encouragement has helped me so much along the way.

And a heartfelt thank you to all of my Indiegogo supporters from my book pre-launch campaign in summer 2012:

Carol Ogden Martin, Alex Martin, Pam Cooper, Brian Rolston, Cassandra Fullarton, Jack Brown, Judy Herilla Lipinski, Nancy Baker Moore, Cathy Dieckman, Christin Cogley, Douglas Hamm, Melanie Carroll, Gretchen Wright, Faith Hershey, Hanan Kallash, Jenn Novik, Brandi Booze, Heather Edwards, Ray Perret, Liezl Perez Schewe, Rory Samantha Green, Deb Johnston, Karla Graves, Pete & Jodi Quint, Page Hunt, Emma Parker, Dave Oatley, Regina Rivers, Angela Nilson, Keith Rajala, Janice Rapp, Cindy Patterson, Matthew J. Mondello, Charlene Kieffaber, Sabrina DeLong, Eric Kovach, Leigh VanHandel, Sherri Rapp, Jenny Bixby, Stephanie Headings, Mary Bynes, Mary Ellen Martin, Laura Harvey, Christy Hiles, Alice Wolfe, Danae Doukas Kenney, B.K. Brimmer, Pamela Vittorio, Jim Martin, Steve Roberts, John & Crystal Martin, Jordan Schmidt, Dan Capone, Kim Hatton, Debbie Carlo, Mike Carlton, Belinda Honigfort, Bryan Canterbury, Adam Schaaf, and one other supporter who was so anonymous that I never figured out who it was!

Without your support, this book might never have been completed! Much love, my friends!

1 ~ Keepin' It Kate: "A New Year, a New Reason to Jump Off a Bridge"

~ January 3 ~

Crappy New Year's, folks!

Oh, don't mind me. It's just been a bit of a rough week.

"Come on, Kate. Surely it can't be that bad," you say.

Well, that's very kind of you. But yes, it can be that bad.

"Why's that?" you say.

You know, the usual. I got fired. My boyfriend dumped me. And I think I may have lost my best friend, too. 'Cause I'm an idiot like that.

Pardon me while I wallow for a moment. **sigh**

Okay, moment over.

On the up-side, I wrote a special poem to commemorate the occasion, just for you, dear Readers. It's a bit late for the Christmas theme, I know, but what the hell. I've messed everything else up lately, anyway. What's one more screw-up to add to the list?

Would you like to read it? You would? Oh, thank you!
Really, you're too kind. I don't know what I'd do without
you guys sometimes. Well, without further ado, here it is:

'Twas three days after New Year's, and all through the house
The bottles were empty, my feelings to douse.
The bills were all stacked on the table with care,
In hopes that some money would soon be paid there.

Alas! There was none, for the cash had dried up,
Since my job I did lose at the store known as Pup.
And I in my sweat pants and looking like crap,
Had just settled down for a post-drinking nap.

When up in my head, there arose such a clatter,
It rattled me! But I knew what was the matter.
Away to that night, my mind flew like a flash,
It tore open my heart, and my nerves it did smash.

'Twas the Eve of New Year's when things came to a head,
And my heart was ripped out, and they left it for dead.
But let me explain just what happened that night,
And you'll see, reader dear, why I'm in such a fright.

The evening began with such cheer and such glee!
On the arm of my man, as glad as could be.
A handsome young lad, and so virile and strong,
I thought I might swoon! What could ever go wrong?

Now Prada! Now Vera! Armani! Dior!
On, Gucci! On, Pucci! On, Chanel! And much more!
The dance floor was swirling with such fine array,
As the young and the hip danced the cold night away.

And then, in a twinkling, my heart hit the roof.
When I nearly committed the year's biggest goof.
The moment when everything first went awry
Was the song where I danced with another young guy.

His eyes—how they twinkled! His spirit, how merry!
Then he whispered sweet nothings that turned my cheeks cherry.
As he drew me in close, my heart started to pound,
But the next thing I knew, he was sprawled on the ground!

I had to escape; I was ready to leave,
But alas, I'm afraid there would be no reprieve.
I raced 'round the club, searching through every room,
'Til at last what I found was my own dismal doom.

I peeked through a door, and my boyfriend I spied.
Thank God! I had found him. I started inside.
When, what to my wondering eyes should appear,
But a ho-ho-ho-HO who was nibbling his ear!

Then came Bachelor Two, and things really got tense,
For that's when the shouting and cursing commenced!
Then laying a fist just below my date's nose,
He turned words on *me*, and my aching heart froze.

What was there to do but to bid them goodbye?
I gathered my things, and I held my head high.
But they heard me exclaim, 'ere I tramped out of sight,
"Crappy New Year's to all, and you all can me bite!"

2 ~ That Guy

~ Ten Years Ago, September ~

"Heads up!" The ball flew past Mitch Reid's head, narrowly missing conking him on the skull. He whirled around to see...of course. That guy.

"Sorry, my bad!" the lanky kid called across the floor with that annoyingly charming grin of his. He'd been charming the whole damned school ever since he transferred in from Lincoln High, and now it looked like he was about to charm his way onto the Senior Varsity squad—even though he was just a freshman. JP Sampson was bad news for Mitch. Great news, on the other hand, for Coach Wadzinski, who seemed to think the sun rose and set from this gargantuan clod's bum. Even now, Coach was hustling over to JP to whisper sweet basketball nothings in his ear.

Mitch plodded over to the bench and took a heavy seat next to the bright yellow cooler, grabbing a paper cup and filling it with water. He turned to find his classmate, Walt, watching him from his usual spot on the sidelines.

Mitch couldn't help but vent. "Three years! It took me three years to make the Senior Varsity squad. I guess I'll be off the starting lineup and back on the bench with you now," he groused.

4

Walt shrugged his indifference. "C'mon, what do you expect? He's half a head taller than anyone else on the team. I'd put him in if I were Coach, too."

Logic did not make Mitch feel any better. It was his senior year. This was supposed to be his time to shine, and he did not appreciate having some stretched-out freshman steal his thunder. He scowled across the court at JP, who continued to practice three-pointers, completely oblivious to the daggers being shot in his direction.

Just then, Mary Beth Taggart popped her head in through the gymnasium door, looking all pert and pretty in her dance squad warm-ups. Strawberry-blonde hair curled in loose waves over her shoulders and down her back, and even from a distance, Mitch could see the bright green of her eyes. She glanced over in his direction and flashed him a quick smile. Just like that, his stomach was tied up in knots.

Walt grinned and poked Mitch in the ribs. "So, you gonna ask her out, or what?"

"Shut up," Mitch hissed. "I'll ask her out when I'm ready." Abruptly, he stood up to rejoin the practice drills.

And that's when JP saw Mary Beth. Mitch gaped as JP loped over to the girl of his dreams and planted a kiss right on her lips. Mitch's feet were frozen to the floor. For just a moment, he thought he might lose his lunch.

Walt crowed with laughter. "I guess you're too late, buddy! Better luck next time!"

It was not a very good year for Mitch.

3 ~ Keepin' It Kate: "Rent?"

~ Five Years Ago, September ~

Are you there, Readers? It's me, Kate.

"And you are...?" [That's you talking.]

Well, it's me. I write this blog.

"Really? That's it?"

Oh, you want more details? Okay, I guess I could do that. How 'bout some lists? Lists are fun.

Heroes: Indiana Jones, Mae West, Mary Leakey, Margaret Mead, T.E. Lawrence, Isaac Asimov, Mark Twain, Sarah Connor (Linda Hamilton incarnation), Old Dan & Little Ann, the Guy on a Buffalo

Anti-Heroes: Heinrich Schliemann, Giovanni Belzoni

Favorite Quotes:
- Never miss a good chance to shut up. - *Will Rogers*
- You only live once, but if you do it right, once is enough. - *Mae West*

- Jealousy is all the fun you think they had. - *Erica Jong*
- If it looks like a duck, and quacks like a duck, we have at least to consider the possibility that we have a small aquatic bird of the family anatidae on our hands. - *Douglas Adams*

Hobbies/Interests: archaeology, history, art, mythology, anything Greek, photography, collecting books, science fiction, word games, men ;)

Poison of Choice: Pimm's No. 1 Cup

"Um, okay. But who the heck are you? Really."

Just your average, run-of-the-mill gal from the Midwest— Berlin Falls, to be exact. Ohiowa State alumna, wicked Scrabble player, and lover of all things ancient and foreign. I have a job. I have a house. Okay, technically, it's a condo. And I have a big chest. (Side note: My big chest used to bother me, but I got over it after a while, and even learned to use the girls to my advantage on occasion. Hey, as Mae West famously said, "Cultivate your curves—they may be dangerous, but they won't be avoided!")

But enough of the Q&A. Now for some free-form thoughts about where the heck my life is going right now, and how the heck I got here.

I work at The Pup is Up. You've probably heard of it: mega-corporation catering to pampered pooches nationwide. I never asked to be a sales rep at The Pup is Up. I'm not really even sure how I got here. No, I take that back. I know exactly how I got here. It started when I graduated college this spring. I had a degree in archaeology fresh in hand, but no idea where to start with this whole "career" thing. What I did know was that I wanted a *break*. After all, I'd spent my whole life toiling away in school. I'd earned the right to take a little time off and enjoy myself before figuring out the whole what-to-do-with-the-rest-of-my-life shebang, right? Well, that's what I thought, anyway.

Roomie and I decided to move off-campus—you know, break away from the old on this grand adventure known as post-college life. I knew I had to find a job eventually, but for the first month or two, well, I guess I was just basking in the glow of graduation, playing the grasshopper in the blazing rays of summer, somehow managing to willfully ignore the fact that things weren't going to be just "taken care of" for me anymore. No academic advisors to nag me about what classes I had to take. No professors to tell me what I had to read and how I should regurgitate it on paper. And most willfully ignored of all, no more bills magically paid through the financial largesse of my ever-obliging parents.

Obliging, no more. On the day we graduated, Dad gave me a big bear hug, a pat on the back, and a check. For a hundred dollars. "The final installment of your college payment plan," he laughed as he handed it to me. "Go out with your friends and have a nice dinner to celebrate," he advised cheerily. Looking down at the check in a daze, it suddenly hit me. This was really it. The end of the mother lode. The gravy train had gone dry...as had my mouth in that moment. What could I say but, "Thanks, Dad," with a sickly smile and an effort to appear non-panicked. Don't get me wrong; I was truly grateful for all my parents had done for me—especially footing the bill for college. Most of my friends were saddled with tens of thousands of dollars of debt already (talk about a rude awakening to the wide, wide world), and I was incredibly glad to have been spared that. Still, it was a shock to think about having to make it on my own—something I'd never given much thought to before.

So there I found myself in late July, lazing by the pool with Roomie on a Sunday afternoon.

She's all like: "Hey, before I forget, rent's due next week."

And I'm all like: "Rent?"

Her: "Yes, rent, dummy."

Me: "Oh right, rent."

Her: "You do have money for rent, don't you?"

Me: *blank look*

That day was the closest I've ever come to seeing Roomie have a hissy fit.

The next morning, I hit the pavement, Roomie's blistering words seared into my brain like a Lazy Kate brand on my heifer ass. Within two days, I found myself at the front desk of a temp agency, blubbering about taking ANY paying job that I could start RIGHT NOW. That's how I found myself stuffing boxes full of packing peanuts and god-awful—or should I say dog-awful—apparel for pampered pooches at The Pup is Up. Temp at first, then full time in just a matter of weeks.

Is this my dream job? Heck no. But it's good enough for now. I've got a slew of new boys to flirt with, and new girlfriends to gossip with over trays of salad and iced tea in the company lunch line, too. And I've got enough money to keep my bills paid. It may not be much, but it's all I need for the time being. Anyhoo, I'll probably get married in the next few years, so I'm not really worried about the long term at this point. So yeah—hooray for my first grown-up, full-time, benefits-having, salary-paying job! I think my parents may even be proud of me.

Welp, until next time, I'm "Keepin' it Kate!"

4 ~ So Much for Pineapple Express

~ Five Years Ago, November ~

The cafeteria at The Pup is Up hummed with the sounds of clacking trays, canned music, and corporate whispers. Mitch put down his half-eaten turkey-pesto on ciabatta. "Come on now. Surely it can't have been that bad." His warm, brown eyes twinkled with amusement.

"Yes, it can," Kate objected, "and don't call me Shirley." They both grinned at the classic *Airplane* reference. If there was one thing Kate Adams loved, it was corny old movies—especially slapstick. "Really, I thought I was going to go out of my mind with boredom. Four whole days with no DVR, dial-up Internet—dial-up!—and nothing to do except sit around and listen to Dad kvetch about his erectile dysfunction and another shitty season for the Lions. What does he expect? It's the fucking Lions. They're only the losingest team in NFL history." She tucked back a strand of chestnut hair that threatened to dip into her salad dressing.

"That does sound like a pretty bad holiday," Mitch conceded. "Old man's still having trouble with the tallywhacker, eh?" He sucked in a long sip of soda through his straw, remembering the unnerving scene from Kate's graduation party when her father had cornered him and described at length (*or rather*, he thought, *not at length*) the pros and cons of using Viagra. "Hell, I can't even smoke pot anymore!" Mr. Adams had complained, detailing how the wacky weed was just a bit too relaxing for certain parts of his anatomy. *Disturbing*, thought Mitch. *But good to know. God, I hope I never have to choose between pot and sex.* His thoughts returned to Kate, who was frowning at the mess of greens on the plate in front of her as she picked through it unenthusiastically.

"Why do I ever order salad?" she said. "I hate salad. I should've gotten a burger. I certainly deserve one after the torture that was Thanksgiving." Her hazel eyes registered disgust.

"You don't hate salad. You're just grumpy because it's the first day back on the job after the holiday weekend."

"You're right," Kate sighed, poking a forkful of arugula into her mouth dutifully. "I don't hate salad. I love salad," she intoned, skeptically imagining that if she said it often enough, she really would believe it. "And you're right. I can't say I was looking forward to coming back here. It just gets so mind-numbing—the same thing on the phone every day, over and over. Nobody ever calls to tell you how happy they are with what they bought. Oh, no. By the time a customer calls me, they're ready to kill someone. The customer is always right? Well, fuck that. Sometimes the customer is just an asshole."

Mitch shook his head. "Thank God I work alone in my cubicle and never have to answer the phone. Work is kinda kicking my ass, though. We've had a lot to do to get the Christmas ad campaigns ready for launch."

Kate nodded sympathetically. "Well, here's something that should help you get through the week. My mom sent you a little care package." She whisked a plastic grocery bag from some secret hiding place and plopped it onto the table, giggling as his face bloomed with delight.

"Pecan tassies?" he licked his lips, already savoring the buttery, sugary goodness of Mrs. Adams' mouth-watering tarts. Kate's eyes flicked to his mouth unconsciously. Not for the first time, she wondered what it might be like to kiss those sensual lips of his. Just because she was dating someone else didn't mean she had to stop looking at other guys, right? Especially a cutie like Mitch.

"Mmmhmm..." she answered in a vampish tone.

"Homemade vanilla buttercreams?" he squeaked, hardly daring to hope.

"Mmmhmmmmmm," Kate purred, her smile broadening.

"And...and..." Mitch was beside himself; he could hardly form a complete sentence.

"And what, Mitch? Say it," she teased, slowly withdrawing from the humble shopping bag the one thing that she knew would send him over the edge. Mitch's hand trembled as he reached for the *pièce de résistance*, wrapped securely in a small foil pan.

"Mine?" he breathed.

"All yours," said Kate with a huge smile, handing it over ceremoniously. "Your very own big, fat slice of homemade caramel pumpkin cheesecake, complete with gingersnap-molasses crust, swirled with toffee bar crumbles, and topped with about two inches of cream cheese frosting."

"Ohhhhhhhhhh," Mitch groaned, his eyes rolling back into his head as he imagined just how good each delectable morsel was going to taste. "Your mom is a goddess!" he declared, snapping up the parcel and inhaling in sheer pleasure.

"I swear," Kate laughed. "I never met a man with a sweet tooth like yours!"

"Well, I never met a woman who could cook like your mom! Her sweets are out of this world."

"I'll tell her you said so," she chuckled. "She likes that kind of hyperbole."

Mitch set the sack of goodies safely aside and resumed eating his turkey sandwich. "So, do you want to hear what my wacky mom did this year? It was a real doozy."

"I'm all ears."

"This year she decided that we were going to make a plaster cast of Butch."

Kate shuddered. "I can't believe you still have that thing around."

"Hey, Butch is our dog!"

"Your dead dog," Kate grimaced.

"Lots of people have their pets preserved."

"Yeah, sure they do..." she nodded her head robotically with a manic smile, making it perfectly obvious that she thought the idea was nuts. "So why did your mom want to make a cast of Butch, anyway?"

"She wanted to use the cast as a mold to make a statue of the dog. Unfortunately, the plaster did a number on poor Butch—fur, you know. A lot of the hair got stuck in the plaster and then came off when she removed the cast."

"Oh, no!" Kate gasped, snickering despite her attempts not to.

"Oh, yes. And she didn't appreciate it very much when I suggested we rename the dog Patches, either." Kate snorted. "So on the one hand, we have this freeze-dried dog, hair falling out in clumps. Looks absolutely terrible. No way we can leave it out in the living room anymore. And on the other hand, we have this nasty plaster cast, furry on the inside here and there, and not a good likeness of Butch, either, for the same reason. Plaster simply wasn't meant to capture the shape of fur. So it looks like Mom won't be able to make the statue after all. She's going to try of course, but I think it's a pretty safe bet that anything she makes with that mold will be a disaster. Let's just hope she doesn't try to cover her creation with shag carpet for realistic effect."

Kate tittered. "Well, at least you probably didn't spend the entire holiday getting grilled by your parents about your dating life. Ugh."

Mitch felt a twinge of jealousy. "And how is the latest walking disaster?"

"Not so good, to be honest. Larry tries, but he's really hopeless. Last week, he had me over for homemade spaghetti. Sounds great in concept, but in execution, not so much. He made the sauce with Boone's Farm. Strawberry Boone's Farm. And the meatballs were totally raw inside, too." She slapped her hand over her mouth, puffed out her cheeks, and made a retching noise as if she'd just upchucked.

"Mmmm, tasty. And let me guess what he served to drink."

"You got it...Boone's Farm."

When they finished laughing, Kate continued. "Not that it really matters whether a guy can cook or not. I know it's the thought that counts. Still, I just don't think Larry and I are going to pan out."

"No pun intended, I'm sure."

Kate groaned, shaking her head and smiling. "What about you? Seeing anyone?"

"Not lately," he admitted. "There's a girl I've got my eye on, though." The look in his eye was decidedly warm, but he turned away before Kate could get a good read.

Kate's heart did a somersault, her lips parting in mild surprise. *Zoiks! Is he flirting with me?* She'd never really given Mitch any serious thought, apart from acknowledging his general level of charm and appeal. She shook her head at her own silly notion. *I must be seeing things. Anyway, it's best to keep Mitch in the No-Fly Zone. I can't afford to lose a friend like him, and I'd be sure to screw it up.*

Unfortunately, sometimes those internal dialogues can become self-fulfilling prophecies.

5 ~ KEEPIN' IT KATE: "ALWAYS A BRIDESMAID..."

~ Four Years Ago, June ~

Have you ever been a bridesmaid? I was for the first time this week. Roomie got married. I suppose I should stop calling her Roomie, since she hasn't actually lived with me for several months now. Let's go with Bestie from here on out. So yeah, Bestie got married, and I was a bridesmaid. No horror stories here; it was a relatively painless day. Even the bridesmaid's dress wasn't so bad: a Kennedy Blue "Chloe" style, in a totally acceptable color of plum that didn't make me want to vomit. (Well, the invoice calls it eggplant, but plum sounds so much nicer, IMO.) Floaty, chiffon skirt cut just above the knee, sleeveless vee-neck with straps so you can showcase the girls without worrying about them popping out (which can definitely be a problem with strapless gowns), and none of those horrible cap sleeves. **shudder** It cost less than $150, and I really could wear this one again. It's a bridesmaid's miracle.

So Bestie got her fairy tale, and I'm totally geeked for her about it. Really! But here I am, still dating duds. And why is it that every single one of them seems to have a dog? As if I don't get enough dog talk around the office at The Pup is Up.

Take Jed, for example. Yes, I went out with a guy named Jed. (I know, what was I thinking?) Jed's your classic redneck: a ball-cap wearin', four-wheel drivin', God-fearin', momma-lovin', flag-wavin', true blue original. Thanks to Jed, I've been able to add "Redneck Dog-Lover" to my list of Men Not to Date. The guns, big trucks, and country music, I can handle. The endless, monotonous Nascar, I can endure. I can even choke down Waffle House when it's absolutely necessary. But Jed's dog was the straw that broke this camel's back.

Here's the thing: redneck men talk to their dogs. You know those deep and meaningful heart-to-hearts that you want your man to have with *you*? Well, they have these talks with their dogs. More than once, I walked in on Jed with his arm cuddled around his (admittedly adorable) beagle, Max. Pouring his heart out about this, that, or the other. But the moment I set foot in the room? He clammed up. The third time this happened, I knew I was licked. You just can't compete with that kind of man-beast intimacy. I even tried luring him away with my best lingerie and a six-pack of Bud. No dice. Dude, if you're passing up screaming hot monkey sex so you can sit on the porch and talk to your dog, we've got a problem here. (That didn't help my ego much, either.)

Then there was Brandon, the "My Dog is the Only Kid I'll Ever Need" guy. First of all, oh sure, you say that now, but when you turn 42, you're going to suddenly realize that, *Hey, I do want kids*, and within six months, you're going to marry some super-cute girl five or ten years younger than you who will be eternally grateful (for at least the first two years) that she will not die an old maid and will at least have a chance to convert some of those raging eggs of hers into little poop-making miracles with her Uncle Herbert's nose and your dad's receding hairline (which, someday, said rugrat will curse you for, fists raised to the heavens, crying out, "Why, oh WHY, was I born into this family of no-hair-having men, dear God, WHY?!?!").

But as I was saying. Brandon. One of his favorite lines was, "Why would I ever want kids when I have a great dog like this?" Sure, Bentley was cute enough—nice personality, loved to play fetch. And I'm only one year out of college, so it's not like I wanna start procreating at this very moment. But I do want kids someday, and logically, I have to assume that Brandon is being up-front when he makes these jokes (that aren't really jokes) about not having kids. And so... sayonara, Brandon!

The silver lining to all these bad dates? At least I've been able to dump these guys before they dump me.

What, did I never tell you about the time the man I thought was the love of my life dumped me on the day of our college graduation? Yeah, that was precious. It still warms the cockles of my heart just to think about it. But that's a story for some other time. For now, I'm off to raise a glass with my gal pals and contemplate why it's looking like I'll always be a bridesmaid, and never a bride.

6 ~ Chapstick and a Toothbrush

~ One Year Ago, June 7 ~

"Are you sure it's okay?" Evette asked anxiously, her voice shaking over the phone.

"Yes, of course," Kate reassured her. "It'll be great to have you as a roommate again. I've missed you! Now get your butt over here and bring your stuff. We'll have you moved in in no time. And believe me, you're doing me a favor. I don't know what I was thinking, buying a condo instead of just renting for a while and saving some money. Money's been tight, so having a little extra income will help me out. It's a win-win." Kate still believed the condo would be a smart investment in the long run, but she hadn't realized the immense feeling of pressure it would place on her shoulders, having to budget so carefully every single month in order to make the mortgage payments. "And anyway, if it weren't for you getting on my ass after college about finding a job, I never would have ended up at The Pup is Up, and I probably wouldn't have my condo now."

Evette sniffled. She'd obviously been crying, something she rarely did. "You're a real life-saver, Kate. I mean it."

"You know I've got your back. Love you, Vetta."

"Love you, too. I'll be over shortly." Evette hung up the

phone.

Poor Vetta. Kate vividly recalled the week Evette Armstrong (at the time, Evette Thomas) had spent moving out of their after-college apartment into Micah's place. She'd sold all of her things. "I won't be needing these anymore," she'd said, "and anyway, there isn't room for them at Micah's place—our place." And now, just a few years later, the marriage was over and Evette was on her own with nothing but the clothes on her back. *Oh, and a broken heart,* she fumed. She supposed Evette would return to using her maiden name now. *She surely won't want to hang on to that asshole's last name.*

Kate shook her head. She had no doubt that Evette would eventually land on her feet, but first, she'd have to dust herself off and start all over again. At least she'd have the summer to lick her wounds before classes started up at Pine Grove Elementary again. *Then again, dealing with a classroom full of fifth-graders might keep her mind off her troubles.* She made a mental note to call Cecie and ask her to come keep Evette company by the pool this summer. The two had been close friends since the day they'd met at Pine Grove, just after Evette's graduation, and Kate knew that Cecie wouldn't fail Evette now.

Kate sat back in the overstuffed loveseat and looked around for a moment in appreciation. She really did cherish her home. She loved the built-in, ceiling-height bookshelves, overflowing with the first-edition books she'd collected over the years. She loved the wood-burning fireplace on cold winter nights, with its crackling glow, campfire smell, and radiant warmth spreading throughout the living room. She loved the back deck that overlooked Raymond Park, a forest of trees crisscrossed with leafy walking paths that went on for miles. Kate took a deep breath and let it out in a contented sigh. Yes, she loved her home and was glad she'd made the decision to buy it, even if it had been a little more "growing up" than she was ready for at the time.

And now Evette was moving in. Kate would miss her time alone. Having the place to herself had been a real luxury. She relished not having to answer to anyone about whether she cleaned the kitchen (though it was usually spotless), how loudly she played her stereo or at what time of night, and especially, the privacy of having visitors over anytime she wanted to without explaining herself to anyone. All of that was about to end, but she couldn't really regret it. *Evette's my best friend, and she needs my help and support now, so that's that.*

Kate stood up, placing her hands on her hips and surveying the living room. It looked ready for Evette's arrival. *Good thing yesterday was cleaning day!* Everything was picked up and in its place, not to mention cleaned, dusted, and vacuumed to a fault. She took a walk-through of the rest of the place to ensure that everything was in order.

Hallway—no problem there. Nothing to keep clean except the carpet, recently vacuumed, and the picture frames, recently dusted. Check. Kitchen, neat and acceptably clean, dishes washed and put away. She would clear some shelves in the pantry and fridge for Evette's use tomorrow. Check. Bathroom, spotless. She took a few moments to clear some space in the cabinet and shower for Evette's things, chucking her own belongings into a plastic grocery bag to deal with later. Check. Her own bedroom, she didn't need to inspect. Evette wouldn't be going in there much anyway. Even so, it was fairly tidy and definitely clean. If there was one thing Kate couldn't abide, it was a dusty room. Dust made her sneeze, so the condo had to stay clean whether she liked it or not.

Kate opened the door to the guest room, which would now be Evette's bedroom, and surveyed its modest furnishings. The hand-me-down, full-size bed frame and mattress had come from her late grandfather's farmstead. She couldn't quite call it an antique, as it was neither old nor especially elegant, but it was solidly built and served its purpose. A small writing desk huddled in one corner, paired with a spindle-back chair. An oversized, cloddish bureau donated by an aunt monopolized the wall next to the closet door. It was something of an eyesore, but once again, it was functional, and beggars couldn't be choosers. Kate was just glad to have enough furniture to fill up the room at all. She wouldn't have been able to afford new furnishings on her own, so she was grateful for the contributions from her family. *It's a pretty room,* she thought. *Evette will like it.* A handmade patchwork quilt in blues and greens decorated the bed, and a few frilly pillows piled at one end added a feminine touch. Mismatched Victorian candlesticks and picture frames adorned the dresser, holding in place the satin runner that draped over the top and down the sides. The focal point of the room was a gorgeous Tiffany-style lamp that graced the wooden desk. The translucent dragonflies and jewel-toned drops of glass cast a warm glow around the room. Wispy curtains of ivory lace finished off the window. Kate pulled the fabric aside to admire the lush trees of Raymond Park behind her home. She smiled. *Yes, Evette will like it. It isn't fancy, but it's home.*

*   *   *   *   *

There was a hesitant knock on the door, so faint it barely broke through Kate's consciousness to rouse her from her wild game of online Scrabble. *Evette!*

She pulled open the door, and sure enough, there stood her best friend, looking far worse for the wear. Her watery blue eyes were bloodshot from crying, and her jet-black hair was a grungy mop of bed-head that looked as if it hadn't been washed in at least three days. She wore a faded mint-green tank top, stained with tiny spatters of what looked like spaghetti sauce and hot fudge, paired with hideous purple sweatpants. Oh, and she was wearing no shoes. Socks, yes—bright fuchsia anklets—but no shoes. From the state of Evette's disarray, Kate knew that her usually impeccable friend was in a bad way, indeed.

"Oh, Vetta!" She hurried her inside and quickly closed the door, then opened her arms. Evette fell into them like a rag doll and started sobbing hysterically.

"It's all right, honey. Get it all out." Kate steered her to the couch and pulled her into a comforting snuggle. Evette's head bobbed against her shoulder as she drizzled a riot of tears down the front of Kate's jersey-knit tee. She moaned and howled like...well, like a woman who'd had her dreams crushed and her heart broken by the only man she'd ever loved. There are some hurts so painful that only physical sounds can get them out of the body, and Evette was practically vomiting her pain into her balled-up fists. She rocked back and forth, curled up in a fetal scrunch. Kate could already hear the edge of raspy rawness in her wailing. She would surely have no voice tomorrow.

Kate stroked her hair, trying to calm her friend with soft shushing sounds. Evette's sobs wound down to an occasional shuddered intake of breath, her frame quivering as air stuttered into her lungs. Kate reached for a tissue and snagged one just in time to intercept the huge snot bubble that threatened to ooze down her ample cleavage. "Blow," she instructed, and Evette honked into the tissue like a champ, completely saturating it. Kate nearly gagged. *Oh, the things I do in the name of friendship.*

"Evette," she said gently. Evette snuffled several times and looked up at her friend with red-rimmed eyes. "Mmmphfff?" was all she could manage, her mouth too dry to form recognizable words.

"Here's what we're going to do. First, we're going to get you into the shower and get you cleaned up." Evette nodded in unresistant agreement. "I'm going to order some food while you're in there. Chinese sound good?" Evette licked her lips and nodded a little more enthusiastically this time. "No hot chilies, I know," Kate assured her. "Then we'll get your things inside and get you settled into your room. Okay?" Evette sank back down against Kate's chest for a moment and breathed out a last long sigh, but Kate felt her head nodding up and down in assent. "Good," she said. "Come on, then."

Kate squeezed out from under her friend and stood up, offering Evette a hand. Fingers intertwined, Kate led her to the bathroom, even though Evette had been there a million times and knew the way perfectly well. She handed Evette a set of fluffy towels from the linen closet in the hallway and a waffle-weave robe she kept for guests, then headed her in the direction of warm, sudsy water and clean, tangle-free hair. It only took a few seconds to place their usual order by app on Kate's smartphone: Mongolian beef, extra veggies for Evette; kung pao shrimp for Kate; an order of crab rangoon to share; and two egg drop soups. *Yum.* Even at the worst of times, Kate could eat.

She stepped outside to grab Evette's things from her car and carried them back to her new room, setting them on the bed. She rummaged through an overstuffed duffel bag until she found some clean pajamas and Evette's sparse cosmetics case. The aged, zip-up case of clear plastic contained only a toothbrush and a tube of chapstick. *Looks like a visit to the makeup counter will be next on the to-do list.* Evette adored her massive assortment of lipsticks, blushes, eye pens, and all kinds of crazy "beauty" implements that Kate wouldn't touch with a ten-foot pole. She had at least two tackle-boxes full of dusts, powders, creams, liquids, glitter, sprays, perfumes, samples, and ten thousand other frou-frou girly things. Kate supposed that she'd left them behind in her haste to put some distance between herself and her soon-to-be-ex-husband. *Maybe I can rescue them from Micah's sometime when Evette is otherwise occupied...*

Kate sat down on the edge of the bed. A flash of metal caught her eye from the duffel bag. A silver picture frame peeked out from amongst the jumble of workout clothes and socks. She reached in and pulled it out, knowing that her friend wouldn't mind. Kate's chin trembled, and her heart squeezed with pain. It was Evette's wedding picture. The bride was decked out in a lovely white gown covered with lace, pearls, and miniature silk flowers. One hand rested on her new husband's arm, her white glove contrasting sharply with his crisp, black tuxedo. Micah was all eyes for Evette, visibly overflowing with love and tenderness for this woman he had pledged to spend his life with. Evette's face glowed with happiness, resembling not at all the sobbing, broken mess of humanity that now occupied Kate's shower.

The water to the shower shut off in the bathroom. Kate was tempted to hide the picture away somewhere, out of sight, but she knew that wouldn't solve anything. Evette had to heal in her own way. *If that means torturing herself with an old photo of happier times, well, I guess that's just what she has to do.* Kate tucked the picture back into Evette's bag. *Besides, maybe she plans to smash it into a million pieces.* The thought cheered her up just a little.

7 ~ Keepin' It Kate: "A Fine Institution"

For those of you following along at home, this week has been a real doozy. The short version is, Bestie (formerly Roomie) just found out that her husband is a lying, cheating bastard, and they're getting a divorce. Oh yes, and she moved back in with me. So now she's Roomie again. Still with me?

Yeah, definitely not something I was expecting. I'm still kind of in shock. These guys seemed like the perfect couple. They were so in love...once. But I guess it takes more than love to make a marriage work sometimes.

It really makes me wonder if I'm cut out for marriage. I've never even come close to taking The Plunge. The longest I've ever made it with anyone was my college boyfriend, and that was only about a year. Gosh, I hate to think how long ago that was. **cringing** (Four years, if you must know.) And anymore, it doesn't seem like I make it past one or two dates with a guy before I find some reason to boot him out the door.

It's a pickle. I'm only 26. By modern standards, I should be free to do whatever, right? Yet it feels like there's always this outdated pressure to find that mythical "soulmate." When I'm "just dating" someone, my friends and family are overeager for me to upgrade my status to "in a relationship." And if things progress to the relationship stage? Inevitably, everyone starts dropping not-so-subtle hints about this guy being "The One." It's ridiculous! Must I be sized up by whether or not I have a piece of man-candy on my arm?

The whole thing just kind of cheeses me off. I didn't spend four years of my life in college to earn my "M.R.S." degree, as my grandmother likes to call it. Nana's been married four times (speaking of marriages not lasting), so naturally, she thinks she's an expert on the matter. She never fails to have some "helpful" advice on how to "catch yourself a man." Well, I've got news for ya, Nana—and for everyone else, too. I'm not interested in catching myself a man.

Okay sure, if some gorgeous Adonis fell into my lap, I probably wouldn't kick him out of bed. I like sex as much as anyone. But finding and keeping a man is simply not a priority at this point in my life—and Roomie's divorce just drives the point home for me. It's like Mae West once said, "Marriage is a great institution, but I'm not ready for an institution."

8 ~ Will that be Glenlivet or Johnnie Walker?

~ Present Day, April 8 ~

Cecilia Marie (Murphy) Tyler looked immaculate, as always. Even at 5'2", Cecie never got lost in a crowd. Her bright red, pixie-cut hair popped no matter where she went. She peeled off her cashmere-lined gloves and neatly closed her dripping umbrella. She unbuttoned her double-breasted, military-style jacket and hung it with care on the hook on the wall. Then she slipped into the booth where Evette and Kate were already waiting.

"Sorry I'm late, guys. I had to drop Brigid off at the library, but she didn't want to get out of bed to get ready. You know how it is..." she trailed off, distractedly fishing her cell phone out of the grandma-worthy purse strapped across her torso. She slid the phone onto the table in anticipation of the inevitable interruptions that continually reminded them that Cecie was a parent first and a friend-slash-person second.

"No worries," said Evette. "You haven't missed anything good. I was just getting ready to grill Kate about her date last night with Mr. Bowtie."

"Ugh, Mr. Bowtie," Kate winced. "Do we have to talk about him before we eat? I'd hate to lose my appetite." She arched an eyebrow and made a face. "Turns out he wasn't just Mr. Bowtie," she said, referring to the online profile picture in which her blind date sported a scarlet bowtie. "He was also Mr. Schnauzer."

"Mr. Schnauzer?" teased Evette. "Another dog lover? You do know how to pick 'em."

"I don't see what you've got against dogs anyway, Kate," said Cecie. "Dogs are great companions—everyone should have a dog! *You* should have a dog," she advised in a matter-of-fact tone, flipping over the breakfast menu to view the daily specials at Norm's Eat-In.

"I think not, thank you very much," said Kate. "And yes, Vetta, another dog lover. This one was a real piece of work. He spent the entire date talking about his dog, Scotch," she rolled her eyes. "We weren't even halfway through the first round of drinks when he pulled out his phone and started showing me this endless slideshow of the dog. Every single photo showed him and the dog on a bunch of boulders. Get it? Scotch on the rocks."

The girls groaned audibly.

"Yeah, that was my reaction, too. 'Look, here's Scotch on the rocks at Red Rocks. Here's Scotch on the rocks at the summit of a fourteen on the Rocky Mountains. Here's Scotch on the rocks at Rock City, Tennessee.' I didn't even know there was such a place as Rock City, Tennessee, but apparently there is, 'cause I saw fifty zillion pictures of the place, dog's eye view. Black and white. Very artistic," she deadpanned.

Cecie wiped away a tear as the girls finished laughing. "Okay, okay, so he was a little dog-obsessed. Maybe he was just nervous and needed to talk about something he felt comfortable with."

"Oh, don't give him that much credit," Kate grumbled. "I'm pretty sure that man was a one-dog show." She winked, and the girls erupted into giggles again.

"Well, I adore dogs," Evette sniffed. "If I were ever going to date again, I'd tell you to send the guy my way." Two pairs of wide eyes turned to her.

"What do you mean, *if* you were ever going to date again?" said Kate. "Since when aren't you going to date again?"

"It's something I just decided recently," she said in a chilly tone, meeting the stares of her friends with a defiant, upturned chin. "You know what it's been like for me since *that day.*"

Kate and Cecie exchanged a glance, remembering "that day" in June, not quite a year ago. It was Evette's third wedding anniversary. That was the day Micah had served Evette breakfast in bed—and then served her divorce papers. *As if the breakfast would cushion the fucking blow. What an asshat.* Kate clenched her teeth and silently fumed, remembering the countless hours she and Cecie had spent comforting Evette in the aftermath.

Even now, poor Evette had to endure Micah's unforgivably happy presence at Pine Grove Elementary, where she taught fifth grade. His new fiancée, Louisa, had a daughter in first grade there, so it was impossible to avoid them. They were there for every pageant, every art show, every parent-teacher conference.

And to think, he met the tramp at the school's Spring Social! Apparently, Micah and Louisa had gotten a bit *too* social during the behind-the-scenes tour. And then Louisa wound up pregnant. Evette was devastated when she found out. It was all downhill to certain divorce after that.

"I've decided that I'm through with men," Evette continued. "I don't think it's in man's nature to be faithful. They simply can't be monogamous. And I...well, I couldn't bear it if a man ever cheated on me again." She lowered her head into her coffee cup to hide the morose tears that welled up in the corners of her eyes. Blinking rapidly and drawing in a breath, she lifted her head again and continued. "Nope, from now on it's going to be just me, myself, and I. And maybe a dog." Her eyes lit up. "Yes—a dog! A man may not be loyal, but a dog sure is." Evette looked delighted with the idea; Kate, less so, since it was her condo they shared.

"So much for monogamy. I guess you'll be mo*dog*amous instead," Cecie wisecracked.

"Yes," said Evette resolutely, then she smiled broadly at her friends. "Modogamous."

"Well then," Cecie raised her coffee mug, "here's to being modogamous."

"Modogamous!" the girls said in unison, knocking their mismatched cups together with the earthy clank of glazed pottery.

Tammy arrived with their order and started offloading plates onto the table with an efficient lack of grace. *Thump*, Kate's bacon and eggs. *Thump*, Evette's fruit plate and cottage cheese. *Thump*, Cecie's sausage biscuits and gravy. *Thump*, a stack of buttermilk pancakes to be split three ways, as per their usual Sunday morning routine.

"Anything else I can get for you?" Tammy asked in a bored voice, already turning away from the table to hustle onward to more pressing tasks.

"How about," Cecie paused, "a scotch on the rocks, all around?" The girls burst into laughter as the puzzled waitress twisted back toward the table and frowned, deciding whether or not they were serious. With an unamused harrumph, she wheeled back around and resumed her course, not to be seen again for the duration of the meal.

9 ~ Drama

~ April 11 ~

Kate closed the front door behind her and slumped against it with relief. It had been a long, long day at work, with one customer complaint after another. All she wanted to do now was sink into the bathtub and enjoy an evening of peace and quiet.

Unfortunately, there was about to be Drama. In the form of a wiggling, wagging, hysterically barking, incredibly ugly, slobbering little chunk of a dog.

And it was jumping on her.

Kate's leather satchel crashed to the ground and she shrieked. Evette came tearing around the corner, wild-eyed, and rushed to grab up the yappity ball of fur. "Kate, stop it, you're scaring him!"

"*I'm* scaring *him*? That thing nearly gave me a heart attack! Vetta, why the heck is there a dog in the house?" Kate scowled, crouching down to gather up the things that had spilled out of her bag onto the floor.

"What?" she batted her eyelashes. "You knew I was getting a dog. I told you." Evette feigned a look of innocence, but Kate knew her well enough to read the mix of confidence and guilt that lurked just beneath the surface. Evette was the kind of gal who preferred to ask for forgiveness, rather than permission. It was one of the traits that Kate loved best about her friend—except when it was used against her. This wasn't the first time she'd been the victim of some such stunt by Evette, and it probably wouldn't be the last.

"When?" demanded Kate, crossing her arms in front of her chest with an exasperated look. "When did you tell me you were getting a dog?" The dog was a pug. *Surely pugs are the ugliest dogs known to man*, she grumbled to herself. Kate examined the puppy, taking in his squashed-up face and light tan, wrinkled coat. His face and ears were pure black, his onyx eyes shining in excitement. His tail, when it wasn't incessantly wagging, settled itself into a neat little curlicue. *Well, that's kind of cute*, she had to admit.

"The other day at Norm's, at breakfast." Evette cuddled the quivering little pug close to her chest, rubbing her own nose against its tiny black one and making soothing shushing sounds. "Awww, precious, did big bad Katie scare you, my widdle angel?"

Ugh, baby talk...revolting! "Oh, come on. I didn't know you were serious with all that stupid talk about mo*dog*amy. We were just humoring you." Kate gauged Evette's expression at zero percent humor.

"Maybe it was all just funny talk to you, but I was dead serious. I'm through with men. It's just me and Drama from now on. And anyway, it's too late to take him back to the shelter now," she said defiantly.

"Drama?" Kate raised one eyebrow.

"Yes, Drama. That's his name." Evette offered the pup in Kate's direction, but Kate flung up her hands and backed away, the revulsion on her face reminiscent of a new father facing his first poopy diaper. Nonetheless, her roommate popped the wriggly little bundle into her arms. He snuffled against her body for a few moments, then looked up at her with his watery eyes, just daring her not to love him. She raised him up to her face, eye to eye. His tiny little tongue flicked out and rasped roughly against the tip of her nose. She giggled and held him away from her. "Hey, that tickles!" she scolded the dog, handing him back to Evette. *He does seem like a nice little fellow...*

Then Kate threw her head back and laughed until her sides started to ache. "Well," she gasped for air between snorts, "with a name like Drama, he should be a perfect fit for you!"

Evette flounced out of the room, taking her furball with her.

10 ~ Keepin' It Kate: "The Trifecta of Suck-i-tude"

~ April 14 ~

You know what sucks? Walking Roomie's dog because she's too hungover to do it. You know what sucks even worse? Walking said dog at six in the morning in the freezing cold—and on a Saturday, at that!

Now, I get it. Roomie has been going through a rough time. Her divorce was finalized last week, and the ex-asshole's new tramp has already had a baby. It's been a shitty year, so I understand why she went out and got hammered last night. But still—she's the one who got the dog, so she should take care of the dog, right?

Anyhoo, the buttcrack of dawn rolls around this morning and what should I wake up to, but a cold, wet nose and a warm, wet tongue making short work of my face. Nasty! Aaaaaand he won't leave me alone. Obviously, he needs to go to the bathroom. Waking up Roomie is not an option, seeing as she's thoroughly passed out, her head hanging over the edge of the bed and trailing drool all the way down to the carpet. Mmmm, attractive. So I have to get up and take Dog outside. Have I mentioned that A) I hate mornings, and B) I hate winter? And as you probably know I'm not a huge fan of dogs, either, so this was the Trifecta of Suck-i-tude.

I take Dog to the park about a block away. And here's where it gets weird. The park is packed with people, and every single one of them has a dog. It's like some kind of alternate universe that us non-dog Muggles have no idea exists. We walk around for a while, my nose numb, my ears blocks of ice, my eyes tearing up from the blistering wind. And then the dog pees on my shoe. Aces!

It's getting light out at this point, and I need to go to work. I grab a drink at the coffee cart, and we start back home. At least my whole face has gone numb now, so I'm not feeling the cold anymore. Snowflakes drift down out of the ever-greens as we make our way out of the park. Walking up the street with Dog, the sound of the snow squeaks under my boots with a satisfying crunch. And I catch myself smiling.

I guess every once in a while, it's not so bad to be up and about early in the morning, even on a cold winter's day. And even with a dog.

11 ~ THE BEST AND THE BRIGHTEST

~ May 5 ~

It had been a hell of a week.

Mitch stared out over the heads of the family members and friends seated before him, knowing he would never get through this speech if he made eye contact with any of them. The people milling about in the back of the funeral parlor were mostly people he didn't know: his father's poker buddies, fellow teachers, old college chums, and a lot of younger faces Mitch couldn't place. Probably his father's students. It was safer to look at those folks in the back, with their restless shuffling and uncomfortable, detached expressions, rather than look into the pained faces of his loved ones. At the edge of his vision, Mitch saw his sister, Tasha, reach out to take their mother's hand. Behind the podium, he dug his fingernails into his palms, trying to suppress the wetness that stung his somber, brown eyes. He cleared his throat and began to speak.

"Miles Franklin Reid was many things to many people. He was a loving husband, a first-class father, an admired teacher, and a mentor to more young people than I can count. He was a classic car buff, a dyed-in-the-wool Cardinals fan, and a *terrible* poker play." The card-playing pals in the back of the room chuckled softly.

"Yes, my father was one of a kind. But we all knew that, didn't we?" A murmur of assent arose from the crowd. "Who else would spend his summers off tutoring the kids who were 'behind' so that they could get ahead? Who else would teach *all* of his kids, not just the boys, how to change a tire, bait a fishing hook, or switch out an electrical outlet?" He looked over at his sister, who acknowledged the comment with a nod. "Who else," Mitch paused, "would put up with my crazy mom and us crazy kids?" He caught his mother's eye; she burst out into a laugh-sob.

"Amen, son!" Mrs. Reid nodded vigorously, the bobbles on her black mourning hat jiggling incongruously for the solemnity of the occasion. She raised a tissue to her nose and gave a loud honk, then wiped her eyes with the back of her hand.

"But no matter how crazy we got, family always came first with Dad. I don't think he missed a single one of my basketball games, or Craig's school plays, or Tasha's track meets. He never once forgot a birthday or his wedding anniversary. In fact, I think he was an even bigger softie about that stuff than Mom." Mitch's heart tightened, and he swallowed back the lump in his throat.

"After us, the most important people in Dad's life were the folks at Fairview High School. He enjoyed teaching there more than words can express. His students meant the world to him." Mitch looked out across the room, scanning the unknown faces. "Anyone here used to be in Dad's class?" he asked. Thirty hands or more went up. Mitch nodded in acknowledgement. "Quite a turnout. I think it's safe to say that Dad meant just as much to his students as they did to him."

Mitch glanced down and scanned to the next notecard, taking a minute to study the words written there, then abandoning the stack of cards on the podium. They were too full of information. People didn't need to hear all that stuff about his dad. They could flip through the photo albums and newspaper clippings in the anteroom if they really wanted to know where he went to high school, or what church he attended. Those details didn't matter to Mitch today. What mattered was the kind of person his father had been.

"When I look back on Dad's life, the thing I remember most is how kind he was. I'll never forget something that happened when I was seven years old. Dad and I were going on our first overnighter with the scout troop, and I was so excited. It was a father-son trip, and I couldn't wait to spend a night tenting in the woods, just me and Dad. We were packing up the car to leave when some lady pulled into the driveway. I didn't really know her; she was someone my parents knew from church. Anyway, she dropped off her son, along with a big pile of camping gear, thanked my dad, and then left. Apparently, Dad had invited some other kid to join us on the camping trip. Travis was his name. He was a year or two older than me, and I'd seen him around school, but we hadn't really met. Dad didn't give me any explanation. All he said was, "Be nice to this boy, Mitch."

"Well, I wasn't very happy to have Travis along for the ride. I wasn't really comfortable around new people. And besides, I wanted Dad all to myself. It was supposed to be him and me, not him and me and some third-wheel. So I sulked the whole way there, while Dad chatted Travis up like they were the oldest of friends. When we got to the campground and set up camp, I wouldn't say one word to Travis, I was so mad he was there. I even put dirt in his sleeping bag." A few quiet chuckles eased the silence in the room.

"Later that night there was a weenie roast at the campfire, and I was finally starting to loosen up and have some fun with the other boys in the troop. Then I noticed that Dad and Travis weren't around. I found them down at the lake, dangling their feet off the end of the dock. My dad had his arm around Travis' shoulders. And Travis was crying." Mitch stopped for a minute and turned his head to one side, clamping his lips together. He filled his lungs with a deep breath through his nostrils, then exhaled in a long breath.

"As it turns out, Travis' father had left his family and

moved across country. Dropped off the face of the Earth, leaving Travis and his mom with no warning and no explanation. I've never felt so sorry in my entire life as I did that night. The kindness in Dad's heart humbled me, and it was a lesson I'll never forget. I slept in a dirty sleeping bag that night, and I never told anyone what I did. Until now." He took out a handkerchief and dabbed his eyes for a moment, pausing to regain his composure before continuing.

"There's no doubt about it. Dad was a special man. Maybe he never traveled the world, or made the headlines of the papers. Maybe he never hit a home run to clinch the World Series. He wasn't the first man into space, or *People* magazine's Sexiest Man Alive. Though Mom might disagree on that one." He met his mother's smile with one of his own. "But Dad was never interested in being 'the best and the brightest,' or racking up awards for his accomplishments. His bucket list only had one thing on it: Be a good man. And at that, he truly was the best and the brightest.

"So today, let's not mourn his passing, but celebrate his life. While my father may have been taken away from us all too soon, it is never too late to learn the lessons he taught. Be kind. Be good. Be happy."

Mitch lowered his head for a moment, leaning heavily against the podium with locked arms. "I love you, Dad. You will be missed."

*   *   *   *   *

The reception at the Methodist Church afterwards was a subdued affair—just family and close friends. The Ladies Aid Society had put together a home-cooked luncheon for the grieving family and their guests. Folding tables groaned under the weight of various pot-luck casseroles, pies, and mayo-based salads of the potato and macaroni variety. The smell of fresh coffee percolated through the air, a welcome aroma to Kate's nose. She poured herself a foam cupful from the tall, silver urn, and got one for Mitch, too. Black, one sugar.

A small group of relatives had gathered around Mitch to offer hugs of condolence and chat in hushed tones about the outrageous cost of funerals, what to do with the sprays of flowers, cremation and living wills, and the various other unpleasant topics people talked about at times like this. Kate handed off the coffee to Mitch and received a look of utter gratitude for her trouble.

"Can I steal you away for a bit?" She put a hand on his arm and tilted her head toward the side door. He nodded.

"Excuse me for a minute, folks." He offered a polite smile and followed Kate out the door.

Evette, Cecie, and her husband, George, were milling about in the parking lot directly behind the church, having just arrived from the funeral.

Mitch sat down heavily on the asphalt curb, his legs sprawled out in front of him, arms draped over his knees. "Thanks for the rescue," he saluted Kate with his coffee cup.

"No problem."

"And thanks for coming, all of you," he looked at each face around him. "It really means a lot to me that you're here. Times like this really show you who your friends are."

"Whatever we can do, Mitch, just let us know," said George in his deep, sincere voice.

Cecie and Evette nodded in agreement. "Yeah, we're here for you, Mitch."

The five friends made small talk for a while about the weather, their jobs, spring baseball training—anything except the funeral. But the reprieve couldn't last forever. A few minutes later, Mitch's cousin Sonya poked her head out the side door.

"Mitch, I think your mother is looking for you. They're getting ready to start serving lunch."

Mitch dumped the rest of the coffee over his shoulder into the grass, and extended an arm up into the air toward George. George pulled him up from the curb with a yank. He heaved a huge sigh, then dusted off the seat of his pants and straightened his jacket. The others preceded him and Kate into the old brick building.

Kate took him by the elbow. "Ready?" she asked softly.

He glanced over at her, the pain in his eyes still raw around the edges. "As ready as I'll ever be. Let's get this over with." The day couldn't end soon enough for him. All he wanted was to be alone to nurse his grief.

But at least if he had to do this, he had Kate by his side. No one had stood by him the way she had, taking care of things for him before he even knew they needed doing. It was she who had made sure his suit was pressed for the funeral today, and she who had stocked his fridge with meals. Kate and Evette had spent the last two evenings sorting through Mitch's extensive digital photo collection and printing off pictures of his father for the memorial table at the funeral parlor. Kate had even helped him figure out what he wanted to say for the eulogy—one of the hardest tasks he'd ever had to face.

Mitch paused before entering the church again, and pulled Kate into his arms, draping his head over her shoulder and leaning into her for support. "I never would have gotten through this week without you, Kate," his low voice cracked. "You're the best friend a guy could ever have." She squeezed him back tightly, tears stinging her eyes.

At last, he turned toward the door, and they started up the steps.

12 ~ Harry's Dim-Sum a-Go-Go

~ June 5 ~

A firm rap sounded on the door. *Ah, hell.* The last thing Mitch was in the mood for was dealing with people. *I'll just ignore it. Maybe whoever it is will go away.* He pulled the fuzzy throw over his head, uninterested in budging from the lazy comfort of his sectional sofa.

The knock sounded louder this time. *Shit.* He allowed his feet to fall over the edge of the cushion, where they plonked down onto the thick carpet with a muted thud. He clutched the back of the sofa with one hand and levered himself up, groaning.

His eyes felt sticky. He blinked a few times and scratched the back of his head, yawning. The sun was setting outside, and the room had become dim. He hit the button on his phone. *8:30. Whoa, did I sleep all day?* Slowly, he stood up and stretched, rubbing his eyes and grimacing at the foul-tasting dryness in his mouth.

"What?" he pulled the door open in annoyance. The coffee-brown hair on his head stuck up in spikes like a bird of paradise, and the skin on the right side of his face sported the indented pattern of the sofa's woven fabric.

Kate took a step back, eyes bugging out in surprise. Instantly, Mitch regretted his surliness.

"Oh, hey, Kate. Sorry. I just woke up from a nap," he said sheepishly. He shrank out of the way so she could come inside, and then flipped on a light or two to brighten up the place.

One glance around the apartment told Kate everything she needed to know. The kitchen was spotlessly stale. Not one dish was out of place; not a scrap of food could be seen. She ventured to guess that the fridge was equally empty and sterile. A grass-woven storage box next to the bare coffee table in the living room was filled with a meticulous stack of unread magazines, still covered in plastic shrinkwrap. And Mitch's work desk and laptop were coated in a fine layer of dust. The only sign of life in the entire room was the rather unkempt, terribly grumpy man that stood before her.

Mitch's brain was still emerging from its groggy fog. "What are you doing here, anyway? Not to be rude," he added in an apologetic tone, scowling at his own bad manners.

"I brought some snacks to gnosh on," she held up a plastic take-out bag from Harry's Dim-Sum a-Go-Go. "It's dinner night. We never miss dinner night."

Dinner night. Mitch had forgotten all about it. *It must be Monday.*

"I take it you haven't eaten yet," she tossed her head toward the No Man's Land of a kitchen, which clearly hadn't been used in some time.

He shook his head. Come to think of it, he probably hadn't eaten all day. He really couldn't remember.

Kate made herself at home, unpacking the copiously stuffed bag onto the dining table. Tangy aromas filled the air as she popped open each white cardboard container. Kate was no dummy; she knew exactly what dishes would most tempt Mitch to eat. She peeled the plastic lid off a large, foam container of hot and sour soup, then plated the seafood pancakes and red bean buns. Out came the steamed chicken and basil dumplings, the pan-fried pork and chive wontons, and the roasted edamame with sea salt.

She turned to present the smorgasbord with a sweep of

her upturned hand. "Chinese comfort food at its best. Dig in."

Mitch's stomach rumbled, and he suddenly realized how very hungry he was. He sat down and started tucking into the food without waiting for further invitation.

"Here. I brought you a bubble tea, too." Kate pulled a lidded cup out of the bag, popped a straw through the top, and set it on the table within his reach.

Mitch tore his attention away from the sumptuous spread and looked over in wonder, as if he couldn't believe there was even more than what had already been given to him. He took a long sip of the icy liquid, its juicy flavors washing over his tongue like a wave of tropical sunshine.

"Mango peach. My favorite."

"I know."

Mitch looked back down at the table, his hands folded in his lap, his head too heavy to lift. "Thank you, Kate. You didn't have to go to so much trouble." His voice was rough with emotion.

She reached out to place her hand over his and answered quietly, "It's no trouble at all."

Unexpectedly, he turned and flung his arms about her neck, a keening cry rising from his throat. She dropped her fork on the floor and clasped her arms around him tightly, holding him close and rocking, rocking, rubbing a soothing circle over his back as his body quaked noiselessly. Hot tears zigzagged down the column of her neck where his face was buried against her skin. She felt the answering tears begin to drip from her own eyes.

After a time, his weeping subsided, and they finished eating in somber silence.

"Why don't you go get cleaned up?" Kate suggested gently, fingering the grubby sleeve of his three-days-worn sweatshirt. "I'll take care of the dishes."

He nodded, sniffling sharply and rubbing the back of his hand across his nose. "Probably a good idea."

Kate quietly cleaned up the remnants of dinner and tucked the leftovers away in his refrigerator. Totally empty, as she'd suspected. *Good thing I brought some groceries.* She fetched in two paper sacks from the car and offloaded a few bachelor essentials into the fridge: heat-and-eat breakfast sandwiches, several pot pies, a frozen pizza or two, hummus, and a big block of cheddar. Oh, and a full cheesecake, New York style. *Mitch does love his sweets.* Into the cupboards went a pound of coffee, cans of soup, peanut butter, yogurt-covered raisins, a box of buttery crackers, a few bananas, and a fresh loaf of crusty Italian bread. She wiped her hands together with satisfaction as she finished up.

The water from the shower shut off, and Mitch stumbled out to rejoin her, looking somewhat self-conscious.

"Well, you certainly look better," Kate smiled warmly. His plaid pajama bottoms and a plain white Hanes were faded but clean, and his damp hair fell loose about his ears in shaggy strands. She wondered for the millionth time how such an adorable, sweet guy could possibly still be single. *He really is cute...*

She shook off the thought and sank into the sofa, stretching out her legs on the long section at the end. "So, you wanna talk about it?" She patted the cushion next to her.

His mouth bunched into a scowl on one side. Then he gave a long exhale, letting the tension drain out of his rigid frame. "Not really, but I suppose I should." He flopped down heavily next to her, unfolding his body down the length of the sofa, and pulled the fluffy throw back over himself. His head settled onto her thigh and he stared off at the wall on the other side of the room. She lifted a hand and softly stroked his hair, waiting for him to speak.

*   *   *   *   *

An abrupt nod of the head shook Kate out of her drowsy state. She glanced over at the reproduction railway clock hanging above the microwave in the kitchen. *A quarter after midnight? Ugh. I must have dozed off.* Her eyes drifted down to the top of Mitch's head, which still rested in her lap, her fingers curled into his hair. He slept.

What a night. She'd known the pressure had been

building up for some time, and that eventually Mitch's stiff upper lip would have to give way. When he'd missed work for the third time in a month yesterday, Kate knew it was time for a depression intervention. Still, even she was surprised at the force of emotions that had come pouring out of her old friend once the floodgates had opened. How much he missed his dad. How he'd died too young. How it just wasn't fair. *No wonder he's sleeping. It must've been exhausting keeping all that bottled up inside.*

He looked so peaceful lying there. She could almost picture him as a little boy, eyelashes curled against his cheeks as his mother tucked him into bed at night. A happy time, long before the pain of his father's loss. He still had something of that boyish air about him, especially in slumber. Gingerly, she brushed a stray lock of hair away from his face. A troubled look passed over his features, and a muffled whimper escaped his mouth as he shifted beneath the blanket.

"It's getting late. I should go," she whispered above his ear.

The words seeped through, but hazily. "Nooooo," he moaned. "Don't go. I don't want you to go..." He reached out and curled an arm around her leg, tucking his fingers beneath the back of her knee.

He must be dreaming... "Mitch," she shook him lightly by the shoulder. "It's after midnight. I should go..."

"Don't leave me!" he wailed, sitting bolt upright, his eyes flared in panic. He clamped his arms around her tightly, hiding his face in the curve of her neck. His body trembled.

Kate's head was swimming as her arms slipped about his waist. The smell of him filled her nostrils; the erratic thump of his heart battered against her chest. His ragged breath trickled down the hollow of her throat and slipped under the edge of her blouse. A shiver coursed down her spine. Somewhere in the background, her rational mind cried out, *Whoa, hit the brakes!* but Kate shoved the thought aside, knowing only that Mitch needed her, and that she couldn't leave him now.

"Shhhhh," she murmured into his ear, cupping the back

of his head in her hands, threading her fingers through his fine hair, scratching his skin in soothing strokes with the tips of her fingernails. "Shhhhh. It's all right. I don't have to go." Lightly, she rested her forehead against his, their eyes closed, breaths mingled.

Mitch's hands moved forward to cradle her face, stroking her cheeks softly with his thumbs. Kate swallowed and drew back a little. She opened her eyes, all defenses down. The message swirling in their hazel depths was clear: *I'm here for you.*

Kate's heart ached. Her dear, dear friend was pining away from grief, and she couldn't bear to see it—not if there was anything she could do about it. She shifted forward, heart racing with trepidation, but feeling in her gut that this was the right thing to do. Before she could second-guess herself, Kate inclined her head toward him and placed a gentle kiss on his mouth. With the healing touch of her lips on his, Mitch's arms locked about her and he drew her downward into the night.

13 ~ BUTTERED BEANS

~ June 6 ~

"Oh, shit!" she bit out, rocketing out of the bed in an instant, pulling on her Levi's before she was even fully standing. *What the hell have I done?*

Kate glanced back over her shoulder at the mostly naked man oozing out from under the covers in the most tantalizing way, then shook herself back into focus. She buttoned up her wrinkled blouse hurriedly, one eye on the bed and one eye on the door, wondering just how fast she could get out of there. *Oh God, nooooo "Morning After" conversation, please!* she desperately beseeched the heavens, hoping she could hit the bricks before Mitch woke up and started asking questions or making puppy-dog eyes or whatever. Last night was not supposed to happen—and now she had no idea what to do about it. She was bad enough at messing up her relationships, never mind complicating her friendships.

Her first boot was halfway on when she heard his sleepy voice behind her. "Hey, where you going?"

She clomped the boot on the floor to force the heel of her foot all the way down faster than it wanted to go, wincing. The second boot started to go on as she heard him wrestle with the covers and sit up. She turned to find him propped up against the downy pillows, leaning back with a contented look on his face.

"Sorry, Mitch, I didn't mean to wake you." It was a time to choose her words carefully, and the fewer the better. He tried to say something, but she continued quickly. "I've got to get back home and change clothes before work. I've already slept half an hour later than I usually do, so I'm going to be hauling ass to get to work on time as it is. We'll talk later, okay?" she tried to sound casual, giving him a hopeful look, all the while silently repeating the mantra, *Please let me go without The Talk, please let me go without The Talk...*

He looked bewildered for a moment, then a cloud passed over his features as if some unpleasant reality had just settled in. She slipped out the door with an apologetic smile before Mitch could say anything further.

*   *   *   *   *

Two words filtered hazily past his hormone-drenched brain: "oh" and "shit." Spoken in a rather emphatic tone. By a female. Something told him he didn't have much time to put two and two together. *Kate!* He felt a moment of elation and couldn't suppress a happy grin.

He rolled over to find her already fully dressed, one boot halfway on, and clearly headed for the door in a hurry. His smile faded. "Hey, where you going?" It was the first thing that popped into his mind to say—anything he could say to keep her here a few minutes longer. Images from the previous night—this morning, if you counted the wee hours—danced deliciously through his head. He still felt her body wrapped around him, still smelled the scent of her on his skin, still savored the taste of her on his lips.

At his voice, her spine stiffened. She turned with a deer-in-the-headlights look and what was, he could tell, a forced smile pasted on her face. "Sorry, Mitch," she said quietly. "I didn't mean to wake you..." He was about to say that he wasn't sorry at all when she rolled over his words with more of her own. Excuses, actually. She would be late. For work. Had to go. "We'll talk later, okay?" It was the *okay* that was the kiss of death for him. He knew that *okay*. That was the *okay* that said, "This is what I want so please don't argue with it." And what she wanted was to be out of there. Now.

It hit him like a blow in the stomach. *She's running out of here.* She didn't want to talk to him, didn't want to see him. Had he been completely wrong about last night? That they'd shared the most intimate, incredible night of each other's life? Well, despite the fact that it'd had such a shitty start and he'd apparently seduced her unwittingly by bawling his face off and clinging to her like a needy child. He wondered for an instant if she'd just been putting on a show of emotion for his sake. *No, she wasn't faking it, not for one second! She wanted to be with me—she's the one who started things.*

Another bleak thought hit him even harder. *It was a pity-fuck. Oh my God. A pity-fuck. How could I not have seen it for what it was?* Kate was just being nice to him— granted, really, really nice—but that was all it had been. *Well, even if that were true, she wouldn't have slept with me if she thought I was a complete ogre, so she must find me at least somewhat attractive. Small comfort, being "somewhat attractive" to the most beautiful woman in the world...*

These thoughts came and went in the blink of an eye as he watched her eyes pleading with him to just let her go without making things awkward. *Just let her go. Sure, I can do that*, he thought a little bitterly. Mitch had seen the occasional one-nighter come and go from Kate's bed, but he never thought it would be him. *I think I'm gonna be sick.* Last night, he'd seen a side of Kate she'd never shared with him before: open, unabashed, deeply loving. And he knew that she had meant it as a gift, no matter how flustered her reaction this morning. Perhaps one night was all he would ever have of Kate. To be honest, it was more than he'd ever expected after so many years of platonic friendship. Perhaps one night would have to be enough.

But now that he'd had a glimpse of the real Kate, Mitch knew that one night would never be enough.

* * * * *

Kate closed the front door as quietly as possible, hoping to duck in and out quickly without running into Evette. Her mind raced, panic not far away. *What have I done? What have I done?!*

Unfortunately, she'd forgotten to factor Drama into the equation. Within seconds, the thunder of wee legs trundled down the hallway, and his eager little face appeared around the corner. Dogdemonium busted loose in a torrent of short, sharp barks and excited circles around Kate's feet.

"Drama, hush!" she pleaded, crouching down and gathering him up in her arms, hoping to silence the squashy-bodied alarm clock. She rumpled the fur between his ears, smiling despite herself at the simple delight that lit up his puppy face.

Too late. Evette appeared, clad in a baby-pink marabou and chiffon peignoir. Even straight out of bed, her roommate had a knack for looking like an old-time Hollywood starlet. Her black tresses curled around her face in sexy waves reminiscent of Rita Hayworth. Kate felt a stab of envy, followed immediately by a bewildered shake of the head. *How in the hell could a man ever leave a woman like that? Just goes to show what an idiot Micah is. He must be up to his armpits in baby poop by this time.* The thought gave her some satisfaction.

"Sooooo," Evette drawled. "Where were *you* last night?"

Kate rolled her eyes and lowered Drama to the floor carefully, patting him on the head as she put him down. He wiggled in pleasure. "Don't get excited, it was nothing. I had a late dinner with Mitch. He was feeling down—you know, about his dad. It got late, and I ended up crashing at his place. No big deal." She hoped that would squelch the topic, but no. It was never so easy with Evette.

"Mmmhmm. You guys have been hanging out a lot lately."

Kate scrubbed her hand over her face, trying to wake herself up. She pinched the bridge of her nose with her fingers. "Oh my God, we are *not* having this conversation again. Of course we've been hanging out a lot lately. It's been a rough month. He's needed a *friend*. And that's just what we are—friends. Last night was nothing." She brushed past her inquisitive roommate on the way to the kitchen, hoping to leave the conversation behind and get a pot of coffee started at the same time.

Evette and Drama followed, hot on her heels. "Last night? Ooooohhh..."

"Vetta, you're exasperating!" Kate doled out coffee grounds into the basket and flipped the red switch on the side of the coffee maker. "You always try to read something into everything. Well, there's nothing to see here, folks, move along. Mitch was a blubbering mess, so I stuffed him full of Chinese food and then sat there and listened until he got it all out. I fell asleep on the couch and didn't wake up until after midnight, so I just decided to crash there for the night. There, are you happy now, Nosy?"

Evette frowned slightly. Kate was more defensive than she ought to be. There was obviously more to it than she was letting on, but Evette knew when to push and when to let things drop. Based on the icy glare she was currently receiving, it was time to let things drop. For now.

"Yes. Thank you for answering my question. That wasn't so hard, was it? Remember, I'm your best friend. Best friends tell each other stuff."

Evette was obviously trying to bait her into telling more, but Kate wasn't going to fall for that. "Did you ever think that maybe Mitch wouldn't want me telling people that he had a complete mental breakdown?"

"Oh please. I'm not 'people.' I'm your roommate—and I'm Mitch's friend, too. And besides, who'm I going to tell that doesn't already know?"

Kate sighed. "I guess." She poked her nose into the cupboard next to the fridge, rummaging for her favorite coffee mug.

Evette finally seemed content to let it drop. "So you headed to work, then?"

"I'm supposed to, ugh. I'm so tired, and we've got meetings all day long. It's going to be miserable. Maybe I should call in sick. I don't need to be in any of those meetings, anyway." *I'm not sure I'm up to seeing Mitch, either...* She sloshed some coffee into her mug and took a long drink, exhaling a grateful "ahhhh" at the taste.

"You should! You never play hooky from work, and you're long overdue for a day off. We could hang out at the pool—maybe see if Cecie wants to join us?" Evette and Cecie had both gotten their Get Out of Jail Free cards when the school year ended the previous week. Cecie still had a few duties to wrap up as school secretary, but her hours were flexible.

"Not a bad idea. It's been a while since we had a girls' day out, and I haven't been to the pool since it opened over Memorial Day." It was the pool area that had finally sold Kate on buying the condo, with its enormous in-ground hot tub and plentiful cushy lounge chairs. "Yeah, let's do it. I could use a day off."

"Schweet! I'll send Cecie a text and see what she's up to." Evette pulled out her phone and tapped out a quick message: *"Something's up with Kate. Wanna help me get to the bottom of it? Headed to the pool..."* She hit the Send button. The response came almost immediately.

"Heck yeah! Meet you at GG tonite? I'm on Brigid duty today; soccer practice."

Evette sent back a quick confirmation. "We're on for later," she told Kate. "She'll meet us at the Gimlet later tonight."

"Perfect. Let me jump in the shower, and then we'll hit the pool."

Evette just smiled, knowing that after a few jet-fuel-strength martinis at the Green Gimlet, if there were any beans to spill, Kate would not only spill them, she would marinate them in butter and serve them up steaming hot on a delicious platter of juicy details.

* * * * *

Several martinis into the evening, Kate's troubles were forgotten and she was singing like a bird. Unfortunately, it was on the stage.

"...these boots were made for walking, and that's just what they'll do..." Kate squawked into the microphone, happily oblivious to her own tone-deafness.

Evette cringed. "Egad, let's hope she doesn't take a stab at Amy Winehouse," she moaned. Cecie tittered, thoroughly enjoying her night out on the town with her two best gal pals, *sans* husband, *sans* six-year-old. Not even bad karaoke (as if there were any other kind) could bring down her mood.

Mercifully, the song ended and the deejay hustled Kate off the stage, despite her attempts to occupy the microphone for an encore performance. Luckily, the crowd at the Green Gimlet was in an indulgent mood. Kate even got a smattering of applause, which would no doubt encourage her to grace to the small stage repeatedly during the course of the evening.

Kate returned to the high-top table, her cheeks flushed with vodka and triumph. "Did you hear that? I was awesome!" she crowed, apparently believing that she actually had, in fact, sounded awesome.

"It was very...entertaining." That was Cecie, ever the diplomat. In all the years the girls had known Kate, they'd never been able to break the news to her that she was a terrible singer.

Kate beamed, already flipping through the giant plastic binder in search of her next recording artist to murder. The waitress arrived to deliver another round of drinks. Somewhere in the shuffle, the binder of songs disappeared, discreetly passed on to a nearby table of aspiring Sinatras. Kate looked momentarily confused, as if realizing something was missing, but not able to put her finger on what it was. Evette quickly turned the conversation in a new direction.

"So, how are things going with your own private Taye Diggs?" she asked Cecie.

"George? Couldn't be better. Do you really think he looks like Taye Diggs? I've always thought he had more of a resemblance to Morris Chestnut, you know, with the mustache and goatee and all." Cecie smiled a little dreamily, gazing off into La-La Land and picturing her handsome husband's dark eyes and electric smile.

Evette frowned as the conversation stalled. Apparently Cecie hadn't taken the hint. "Really, what's new with you guys? There must be something you've been up to that you could tell us about," she prodded.

Cecie's face was a blank, the wheels turning in her head but coming up with nada. Then she giggled. "Well, there is one thing, but you might not want to hear about that."

"Nooooo, go on!" Evette pressed her friend.

"Um, okay." She laughed nervously again before continuing. "George and I have been doing these, um, workshops lately."

"Workshops?"

"Yeah. Here, hang on, I'll show you." Cecie poked at the screen on her phone and brought up a webpage. She handed the phone over to Evette and Kate.

Kate's eyes boggled as Evette read aloud from the page. "Intimate Play. Could your sex life use a boost? Looking for that playful side of your relationship again? You've come to the right place! At Intimate Play workshops, you and your partner will rekindle those magical moments that used to come so easily in your relationship. From Oral Sex to Orgasms, Anal Play to (Erogenous) Zones, we'll cover aspects of erotic play that you never even knew existed. So get ready to rev up your joy-toys, folks, 'cause you're in for one wild ride!"

Karaoke was now seriously forgotten.

"Cecie! Really?!" Kate exclaimed. "I never would have thought...!" She barked a short laugh, then the incredulous look on her face shifted to one of concern. "Are you and George okay? I mean...I thought you guys were good in that department..."

Cecie jumped in hastily. "Oh, we're fine! The marriage is fine, the sex life is fine," she reassured her friends. "But hey, every relationship can use a little spice once in a while. We've been married for nine years now, and it's true what they say. It takes work to keep the love alive."

"What kind of things do you do in these workshops, anyway?" Kate asked eagerly. "Or maybe we don't want to know?" she joked.

"We don't *do* anything at the workshops—not *that*, anyway. We mostly talk about different things we can do at home with our partner."

Evette's curiosity got the better of her. "Like what?"

"Well, the first week we went, the group started with something simple—role play. That was pretty revealing. Each of us had to write a secret fantasy that we've never told our partner, then we all put them into a hat. The instructor read them all aloud, one at a time. Gosh, I was so embarrassed when she read mine to the class. Thank goodness our names weren't on them!"

"What was it?" Evette elbowed her in the ribs.

"I'm not telling you that! But boy, there were some real doozies—stuff I never would have dreamed of. We had to write them all down in our notebooks, too. Food for thought, I guess. The most uncomfortable part was trying to guess which one was George's."

"Did you guess it?" Kate asked.

"No! That's the awful part. He didn't get mine right, either. But you know, it was good for us. We haven't had been that frank with each other about sex since before Brigid was born, I think."

"So then you were supposed to try out your secret fantasies at home?"

"Actually, we picked someone else's. It sounded like so much fun..." Cecie blushed a little. "The Genie and the Harem Girl," she admitted. Kate and Evette cackled with glee.

"Oh, brother," groaned Evette, "I'm pretty sure I don't want to hear this one!"

"Hey," protested Cecie, "it was a lot of fun. A genie is all-powerful, so you can wish for whatever you want."

"And what did you wish for?" Kate teased.

"All kinds of things! Body servants to wait on me hand and foot, a tropical island paradise, our own personal musicians playing soft, romantic melodies, and of course, a great big bed, piled high with ten zillion silky pillows. George described every single thing in perfect detail as he granted my wishes, one by one. It was all so beautiful, I could almost believe it was real."

"Sounds like it was all about you," Evette observed. "What about George? What did he get out of it?"

Cecie snorted. "Are you kidding? The idea of being all-powerful went straight to his head. He had a ball with it. Ahem...no pun intended." She smiled coyly. "But you know what else? It got us thinking about how we make fantasies like that come true for real. We can't really make wishes or fly on magic carpets, but we figured out that we *can* pamper each other a lot more than we do. We've been so busy in the last few years with Brigid that we've hardly taken any time for each other. So we decided to take a vacation, just the two of us."

"That's wonderful!" Kate smiled genuinely at her friend.

"Yeah, I can't wait. We booked a room in Miami at this crazy hotel for couples only. They even have a suite with an Arabian Nights theme, so of course, we had to get that one." She grinned. "We plan to reprise the roles of the Genie and the Harem Girl while we're there."

"Awwwwww! You're so lucky you have George," Evette sighed, a touch of melancholy in her voice. Cecie reached across the table and covered her friend's hand with her own.

"Yes, I am. And you're going to find a great guy, too. I just know it."

Evette shrugged. "Mmm, maybe. But I think I'll just stick with my dog for now. Drama is all the man I can handle at the moment. And anyhow, he never dips into my stash of emergency chocolate, like Micah always did."

The girls laughed. Evette offered a slight smile, warming up to the conversation. "He doesn't snore or hog the blankets, either," she joked.

"I'm glad that whole modogamous thing is working out for you." Kate leaned over to Cecie with a loud whisper behind her hand, "I guess this wouldn't be a good time to tell her I've been sleeping with Drama, too, eh?"

Evette smacked Kate in the arm with a light backhand. "Ha ha ha, very funny. And don't think I haven't noticed Drama sneaking off to your room every now and then. I'm surprised you haven't kicked him out."

Kate shrugged. "What can I say. He's not so bad in bed," she winked.

And that's when Evette saw her opportunity. "Probably not as good as Mitch, I suppose," she said in a casual tone.

Kate's head snapped up, her eyes wide. A crimson blush blazed up her neck to cover her cheeks. *Shit, ambushed!* Her embarrassment was instantly replaced by fury. "Vetta! That's none of your damned business!"

Cecie's head whipped in Kate's direction. "Really?! Oh, Kate, that's great news! It's about time!"

Kate slapped a hand over her eyes and leaned forward onto the table, shaking her head back and forth as if the motion could erase the last sixty seconds from existence. "Stop. Just stop right there," she said, glaring at her two friends. "I don't want to talk about it."

"So it's true then—I knew it! Come on, Kate, this is great news!" Evette grabbed her arm.

Kate pulled her arm out of Evette's grip with a jerk, shaking her head emphatically. "How is this great news? We very likely fucked up years of friendship in one huge mistake of a night."

Cecie touched her hand to her throat with a look of concern. "What, it wasn't good?"

Kate looked offended. "Oh, it was good." *Damn, was it good...*

"Did you have a fight, then?"

"No, we didn't have a fight."

"So what's the problem?"

Kate looked bewildered. "I don't know. I guess I've never really thought about Mitch in that way. And I certainly didn't intend for it to happen. I went over to his place last night with some takeout—he hasn't been eating, you know, and he's been missing work. I've been worried." Her eyebrows knit together. "Then out of nowhere, he started crying, and then I started crying, and then he got to talking about his dad. I don't know how long that went on—an hour, maybe? All I know is that I woke up on the couch and he was asleep in my lap, and when I tried to go, well, he asked me not to." *Begged me not to.* Her mind filled with the heartwrenching sadness in Mitch's eyes, the desperation in his voice. "And then, well, you know what they say. One thing just led to another." Kate slumped onto the table, pushing away her empty martini glass.

Evette looked hopeful. "This is not necessarily a bad thing, Kate. Maybe it's just giving both of you a nudge in the right direction. Mitch is an awesome guy. You know that better than anyone—you two are so close. Maybe this is the start of something really good."

Kate reached across the table and took a big swallow of Cecie's martini. Cecie never finished her drinks anyway. "I don't know. Like I said, I never really thought of Mitch that way. We all know that Mitch is great, sure, and yeah, I love him to pieces, but as a *friend*. It's not like you can turn those feelings on and off. I feel horrible. It never should have happened; he was too mixed up to think straight. I almost feel like I took advantage of him."

"Took advantage of him? I thought you said things just happened." Evette looked at her in concern.

"Yeah, well...I may have been the one to start things," Kate admitted glumly. "He just looked so damned *miserable*, and so damned...cute. Ugh!!! I just hope I haven't screwed our friendship up completely."

"Have you talked to him about it?" asked Cecie.

"No. That's kinda why I skipped work today—so I wouldn't have to face him. I know it's not very mature of me, but I don't know what to say to him. I guess I thought I'd give it some time to see if things blow over. He's sent me a text or two, but I haven't known what to say, so I haven't answered them."

Evette frowned. "Not cool, Kate. Not cool." Kate scowled at her but didn't respond. "So you're not interested, then? Or you just don't know if you're interested? 'Cause if you're interested, you really shouldn't let this blow over without at least trying to see if there's anything there. Or maybe you're just being a chicken shit," she ventured, none too gently.

"Easy for you to say; you've got nothing to lose here," Kate snapped back. "It's just too complicated. Mitch and I have been friends for too long. Last night was a one-time thing, I guarantee it. So do me a favor, and let it drop."

Evette persisted. "All I'm saying is that if you haven't seriously considered a relationship with Mitch, you should. You've already done all that getting-to-know-you crap, and you know that he's a super guy. You've seen each other at your worst, and you're still friends after all that. If there is some kind of connection there, you should give it a chance. Don't just blow it off because you don't know what to do about it."

Kate crossed her arms, her jaw set. "Are you finished?"

Evette sighed. "Yes, I've said what I have to say."

"What about you, Cecie? Got anything else you need to say?" Kate bristled.

"Only that I think Evette may have a point. Give it some thought before you decide what to do, okay?" Cecie hated confrontation of any sort, so Kate knew how hard it was for her to give an unwelcome opinion.

"Fine, whatever. Now if we're done with the cross-examination, I'd like to move on with the evening. Where in the blue blazes did that binder go, anyway?" She lurched from the bar stool, on the hunt for the songlist and out of the line of fire from her well-meaning friends.

"We're in for it now," Cecie shuddered.

14 ~ A Friend-Sized Mack Truck

~ June 7 ~

Kate scanned the cafeteria for any sign of Mitch. It looked like she was in the clear. She thought about just grabbing a sandwich and hightailing it back to her cubicle. *It's only 11:30. He's never down here this early.*

She scoped the room for an empty seat and found one in an out-of-the-way corner, where a gaggle of Chatty Cathies were gabbing over their chef salads and club sandwiches. Kate slid into a chair at the end of the table, receiving a few odd looks from the group since she wasn't one of their usual crew. Nonetheless, she was welcomed by one or two with a nod. Quickly and quietly, Kate tucked into her grilled cheese, hoping to make short work of it and get back to her desk.

No such luck. She could feel his eyeballs boring into the back of her skull before she even turned around. She furtively peeked over one shoulder. Sure enough, Mitch was staring at her from the double-doorway entrance to the room. She tried to pretend she hadn't seen him.

It didn't work. Seconds later, he was standing next to her at the end of the table, his hands fidgeting in the pockets of his Dockers. Grey, flat front. Very flattering, actually. Kate had a sudden mental picture of Mitch without any pants on at all. And here he was, his *you know*, just inches away from her face. She blushed, mortified at the heated turn her thoughts were taking. She shook her head slightly so that her hair would rustle down around her burning cheeks, trying to shield her expression from both Mitch and the others at the table.

"Hi, Kate." Curious eyes turned their way.

"Hi, Mitch," she said. Friendly, but not too friendly. "Did you need something? I'm on my lunch break." *Oh, hell.* That came off way more distant than she'd intended, as if he were merely some office annoyance that she had to deal with at an inconvenient time, rather than one of her closest friends.

He blanched. "No, not at all. I just wanted to see if you were okay. I noticed you weren't at work yesterday, and I thought you might not be feeling well."

"Oh, I'm fine. I just had a bit of a stomachache," she fibbed. Stillness settled uncomfortably between them.

"Well, I don't want to keep you from your lunch," he mumbled. "I'll see you around." He slid away without another word. The table, which had fallen mostly silent, shrugged and resumed their low buzz of chit-chat and potato-chip crunching.

Ugh! Stupid, stupid, stupid! If Kate could've kicked herself in the ass with her own foot, she would've done it. She really hadn't meant to be so curt with Mitch. *Damnit, why couldn't he have just given me a bit of space?* She still wasn't sure how she felt about what had happened the other night. Did she care for Mitch as more than a friend? Maybe...she just didn't know. *But now he probably won't want to have anything to do with me. Once again, I've screwed things up.* As if the way she'd left him in the dust yesterday morning wasn't bad enough.

* * * * *

Kate sat at the far side of the cafeteria, surrounded by half a dozen of the noisiest, nosiest ladies in the whole company. Mitch frowned. He just couldn't catch a break.

He'd been useless all day yesterday at work, and all day

today, too. His head was filled with steamy visuals from his night with Kate, followed by newsreels of her devastating departure. Thank goodness he worked on his own, safely tucked away in an isolated cubicle where he was unlikely to be disturbed except in the event of a graphic design emergency.

After about an hour of mucking around on his computer and trying in vain to get some work done, Mitch finally gave up. He pulled out his drawing pad. Sketching was one of the few activities that could snap him out of a funk. The pointed tip of lead frosted gently over the white sheet, leaving behind a soft, grey trail of magic. Mitch allowed the pencil free rein and found a tranquil landscape emerging, filled with arrow-straight tree trunks and barely-there clouds. A glassy lake came to life, and the tip of a rowboat broke the plane at the bottom of the page, as if the viewer were sluicing forward into the sketch, one paddle-stroke at a time. All the while, Mitch's mind was going over scenes from the last 48 hours, trying to make sense of what had happened.

Mitch couldn't deny that he'd always had a bit of a thing for Kate. The timing, though, had always been terrible. When they'd first met in college, she'd been dating Vance. Then when Vance broke up with her, it was Mitch who was off the market. And by the time they were both single, they'd already passed through that delicate period during which two people either become lovers or settle into being mere friends. So there he was, stuck in the Friend Zone. Trying to get out, however un-successfully. He'd never been good at putting himself forward when it came to women.

Observing her from across the cafeteria, he hesitated. She'd made it clear yesterday morning that she didn't want to talk. He understood her need for a little distance—especially since he had no idea what to think about the situation himself. This wasn't the right place or time for "The Talk" anyway. But at least he could offer a quick hello and a friendly smile, just to make sure that things were cool between them.

He was halfway across the room before he realized his

feet had started moving. Inwardly, he balked. Facing Kate in front of all of these people—co-workers, especially—was a daunting task for a man of his reserve. But they had to break the ice sometime. *It's only hello. Even I can't screw that up.*

"Hi, Kate." He spoke quietly and, he hoped, warmly. As she glanced up at him and their eyes connected, he caught the memory of her lovely face flushed with pleasure. The thought crippled his barely functioning mind, and his ears scarcely registered her response.

"Hi, Mitch," he heard her saying. "Did you need something? I'm on my lunch break."

Whatever air had been inflating his hopes hissed out in a *sssssss* of disappointment. *Really, that's all she has to say to me? As if I were some guy she barely knows?* He was astounded. Confounded. And every other *–ounded* word he couldn't think of at the moment. *Who does she think she is, anyway?* He bristled at her "just co-workers" tone, wounded by her aloofness.

But Mitch could sense the many ears at the table tuned their way, as if searching for the Juicy News frequency. The last thing he wanted was to be the talk of the office.

"No, not at all," he replied coolly. "I just wanted to see if you were okay. I noticed you weren't at work yesterday, and I thought you might not be feeling well." Somehow, the conversation finished itself, and he strode away from the table and out of the cafeteria without looking back.

*   *   *   *   *

"Mitch!" Kate called out, pursuing him across the parking lot as he headed for his car. He had to have heard her; he wasn't that far away. But he kept walking. "Mitch!" she called again, louder this time. She saw him break stride just a hair, but he kept going, not looking back. By the time she caught up with him, he'd already pulled out of his parking spot and was getting ready to throw the stick shift into first gear.

She positioned herself in front of his car, blocking his getaway. He sat in the driver's seat, clutching the wheel at ten and two, engine idling, glaring at her through the windshield. He rolled down the window and spoke in a calm, clear voice. "I highly suggest you step aside, as you're standing in the spot where I'm about to be driving in ten seconds."

Ouch. "Can we just talk for a minute, Mitch?"

"You talk, I'll count. Ten. Nine..." He revved the engine just a smidge.

"Oh, come on!" Kate splayed her hands on the hood of the car, looking slightly alarmed. "Look, I'm sorry about how I acted at lunch..."

"Eight. Seven..."

"I didn't mean to come off like that..."

"Six. Five..."

"You just caught me by surprise!" she shouted over the snarl of the engine.

"Four. Three..."

It seemed that he was serious. The car rattled hotly under Kate's hands, but Kate wasn't about to back down. She met Mitch's glare with a look of determination and balled her fists on her hips. "I'm not going anywhere until you talk to me!" she shouted.

"Two. One!" Mitch shifted into reverse and pulled away, dismissing Kate with a curt salute as he hit the gas. Just like that, he was gone.

*   *   *   *   *

Let her stew, Mitch thought with some satisfaction. *She's earned a little angst.* It wasn't his usual nature to wish anyone ill, but Kate's chilly behavior in the last two days had stripped away his mild manners for once. He wasn't sure where the tires were taking him just yet. All he knew was that he wanted to get away. He turned the wheel eastward and headed out of town, just driving.

But it was him who couldn't stop stewing. The more he thought about getting involved with Kate, the less it seemed like a good idea. *It's obvious our night together didn't mean the same thing to her that it did to me.* Not to mention her horrific behavior of the last 48 hours:

abandoning him the morning after his breakdown, skipping work, not answering his calls or texts...*If Kate's as messed up with other men as she's been with me, well, it was no wonder she's single.* His chest ached. He was beginning to understand why women barricaded themselves in their apartments for the evening, dragged out the pints of Ben and Jerry's, and bawled their way through *Steel Magnolias.*

Mitch scanned the two-lane country road before him, emerald trees waving leafy fingers toward the sky as he sped past. It seemed that he had found a destination: the cemetery. His tires crunched over the gravel as he turned the car into the entrance and slowly crept up the lane toward the family's burial plot on top of the low hill. The car door echoed as he banged it closed, its reverberation carrying through the still air of the valley.

Cemeteries had never bothered Mitch; he rather liked them, in truth. He trudged through the moldering headstones toward the collection of graves that held the rotting bones of his ancestors. As he walked, he scanned the headstones and deciphered the names of the people who had come before, thinking about the things they must have seen in their lifetimes.

He came upon his destination. The brown earth mounded up on his father's grave had settled into a flat bed, and grass had begun to sprout. A spray of flowers rested next to the headstone, browned and curling at the edges. Mitch removed the sad arrangement, making a mental note to return on the weekend with a fresh bouquet to replace it.

Now that Mitch was here, he wasn't sure why. He studied his father's gravestone. *Miles Franklin Reid, July 24, 1950 – May 2, 2012.* On the other half of the double stone was his mother's name and date of birth, *Regina Ann Reid, Nov. 28, 1952 – .* An unetched spot awaited the date of her demise. Now *that* was depressing. The last thing Mitch wanted to think about was losing his mother.

He turned away from the grave, shoving his hands in his pants pockets. Strolling around the family plot, he read off the names of his ancestors: Beulah McCormick, grandmother; Harold Mason Reid, great-uncle; Anita and Marcel Reid, grandparents; Quinton and Ruthanne Cole, great-grandparents. Cousins from his grandparents' generation, and even a few from his parents' generation, lay buried there, too: Dionna and Donnell Dreier, Kendrick Mason, Edward "Eddie" Dreier, Jolene and Teresia Wanabaker. As he passed by the gravestones, memories of each person surfaced. Some, he had only met a few times at family reunions during his childhood. He smiled, remembering those carefree summer outings. Playing with his cousins in his grandfather's grassy fields. Sneaking sodas from the iced cooler beneath the oak tree. Popping open the glass bottles with the metal church key that dangled from one of the limbs by a string. Tables set up on the lawn, loaded down with casserole dishes and more homemade pies than any fifty people should eat in a year. *Good times, good times...*

Mitch came round to his father's plot again. He placed a hand on top of the smooth stone, running his fingers over its slick newness. His mind was a blank. If there was something needing to be said, he didn't know what it was. Perhaps it was enough that he was simply here, paying his respects and holding his father in his heart. *I miss you every day, Dad.*

He turned away and slowly retraced his steps to the car, pausing for a moment to turn back and gaze at his father's gravestone one more time. *Well, Dad, if you are up there in heaven looking out for me, see if you can keep the crazy women away from me, would you?*

Speaking of crazy women, he supposed it was time to face the music with Kate.

* * * * *

7:45. Kate was early. That was fine, she didn't mind waiting. She was just glad Mitch had returned her text and agreed to meet. Her stomach was in knots. *What the heck am I going to say to Mitch when he gets here?*

The Den wasn't her favorite location, either, which didn't help her anxiety any. It was a guys' bar—not really her kind of place. A grubby-looking man at the end of the bar was eyeballing her like she was a plump, juicy pot roast. She ordered a diet soda from the bartender and quickly scoped the room for an out-of-the-way place to sit.

Her mind drifted back to the day she and Mitch had met. She and then-boyfriend Vance were at a friend's birthday party when Mitch walked through the door. He was handsome, but quietly handsome. Not one of those guys you would pick out in a crowd as drop-dead, but definitely someone you'd take a second look at if there weren't any drop-deads around. Very lean, and moderately tall—probably six foot—with slim-fit jeans hugging his hips and legs. Straight brown hair, shaggy cut, almost hiding his face. Brown eyes, long lashes, thick eyebrows. Not quite five o'clock shadow dusted his jawline—more like three o'clock scruff. Just enough stubble for Kate to wonder what it might feel like if he grazed his chin across the hollow of her neck, following the curve up toward the base of her ear with all that scratchy, scruffy goodness. *Mmmm...* The hair on her arms stood up just thinking about it. All in all, a pleasing sight to a warm-blooded female's eye, Kate had concluded at the time...and thought so ever since.

And now I've slept with him. And made a complete botch of it. What's wrong with me, anyway? Even when a good thing comes my way, I fuck it up.

The diet swill in her glass was singularly unsatisfying. She wished she'd ordered something a bit stronger. But before she could follow those thoughts to their alcoholic conclusion, Mitch appeared in the doorway. His mouth was still set in that grim line that had been in place when he'd peeled out from the parking lot at work a few hours earlier. Kate's nerves jangled. *Looks like I've got my work cut out for me.*

Mitch spotted her at the secluded table she'd chosen in one corner, a darkish space populated by no one, and wound his way through the tables and chairs to join her.

"Tequila," he flagged down the waitress before she had a chance to ask. "Two Patrons. And two of whatever's on tap to chase it. Thanks." He was all business.

So there they were. Sitting in silence across from one another in a dimly lit bar.

The shots arrived.

"Down the hatch." Kate lifted her glass resolutely, then knocked it back in one swift gulp. The trick with tequila, she'd discovered, was to keep the burning liquid from touching her tongue. If she couldn't taste it, it wasn't that bad. *And hey, at least it's a drink.* A shiver shot down Kate's spine as the alcohol hit her stomach, fortifying her resolve. *Welp, I may as well not mince words. Here goes nothing.*

"So did I mention that I'm a total jerk?" She was met with a sardonic half-grin. Mitch leaned back in his chair, arms crossed, waiting for her to continue.

"Look, I'm really sorry about lunch today. You caught me off guard. I didn't really want to talk in front of all those people..."

"And you think I did? I just came over to say hello, and instead I got the freeze-out."

"You're right. I'm really sorry." Kate stared down at the floor, crossing her arms over her stomach and swallowing.

He let out a low sigh. "Fine. Let's just forget about it."

She nodded gratefully. But the hardest part wasn't over yet. The elephant in the room was trumpeting in her ear. "So I guess we should talk about...what happened."

"Yes, I suppose we should."

Kate supposed it was up to her to get the ball rolling. "Well, first of all, let me ask if you're feeling okay, now. About your dad, I mean."

Mitch took a long sip of the chilled beer in front of him, then nodded his head slowly a few times. "Yes," he said, sounding a bit surprised. "I guess I do." The tension in his shoulders eased a bit. "I just came from the cemetery, actually. That's where I went after work."

Kate knew that Mitch hadn't been back there since the funeral. She wished she could reach out and take his hand, but then thought better of it. "How'd it go?"

He tilted his head back and scrutinized the ceiling. His hands joined together behind his head, thumbs massaging the tension at the base of his skull. A stray lock of hair fell across his dark eyes, and he huffed it away with a quick breath. "Good. It was good."

That seemed to be all he had to say on the subject. And that damned elephant was still sitting there, tapping its toenails on the table and staring her down relentlessly. Kate rubbed her hands over her face and exhaled. *Ugh, this is so hard.*

"So..." she drawled, delaying the tough question they'd been avoiding. "Anything we need to talk about in regards to, you know..."

"Yes, yes, I know," he saved her from completing the thought. "I'm not sure. Do you think we need to talk?"

"Maybe? It seems like something people usually do after they've, um, been together." She paused. "Have you been tested recently?"

"No need to. I haven't been with anyone since Camille."

"Wow, really?" Her voice was incredulous. Mitch looked somewhat offended. "Sorry," she apologized quickly. "It's just, that's been more than a year."

He shrugged. "What about you? Clean?"

"Certainly."

"Birth control?"

"*Most* certainly."

"Good," Mitch nodded, not sure what to say next. He considered all that had happened since that night. How fast Kate had scooted out the door the next morning. How she'd been avoiding him at work, and not returning his texts or emails. And how distressed she looked at the moment, wringing her hands and biting the inside of her cheek.

Mitch knew Kate cared for him, but she definitely didn't look like a woman "in crush" with him. In fact, she looked quite wretched. In that moment, he knew something with certainty. *Kate doesn't have those kind of feelings for me, no matter what happened between us.* The thought pained him, and his vision blurred for an instant.

Logical thought took over again. *What if it were me? What if she loved me and I didn't love her back? I'd do whatever I could to keep from hurting her feelings—to keep our friendship intact.* The kindest thing to do would be to let her off the hook. He could already see the writing on the wall; there was no need for her to spell it out.

Kate opened her mouth to speak, but Mitch took the lead. "Maybe we shouldn't overthink things," he suggested. "You know, put too much significance on them. What happened, happened, and it's done."

"Oh." Kate felt the words like a blow to the gut. *He's sorry it happened. I should never have gone over there.* Her throat closed up, and she felt like she'd never be able to breathe again.

Seeing the distressed look on her face and mistaking it for embarrassment, Mitch quickly jumped back in. "Don't take that the wrong way—it was a great night," his cheeks rouged noticeably. "Really great," he said more softly. "But maybe it's best if we just leave it alone...move on. As friends. I'm in no state to be sorting out emotional baggage right now. I'm kind of a train wreck, in case you haven't noticed." His expression was both wry and apologetic.

"Sure." Kate pulled her wits together as rapidly as she could. *It was great...really great...no state for sorting out emotional baggage...* Pictures flashed in her mind of the night they'd spent together...*move on, as friends...* him looking down at her like she was an angel incarnate...*really great...*arms wrapped around each other, kissing, and kissing, and kissing, and kissing...*better not to overthink things...*

Her head was spinning. She felt like she needed to get out of there. Right. Now. But she knew that she couldn't. Scurrying off would give away her hand; she had to bluff her way through this one and then hit the bricks as soon as she could get away without suspicion. Without him suspecting, that is, that he'd just effectively run her over with a friend-sized mack truck. *All this time I've been worried that he might have taken things the wrong way, or that I might have hurt him even more. Turns out that I'm the one making too big a deal out of everything. He doesn't want me. He wants to forget it ever happened.*

"Sure," she repeated. "Friends. Yes, of course. I'm so

glad you feel the same way," she mouthed the words that she thought he wanted to hear, the taste acrid on her tongue.

15 ~ Keepin' It Kate: "A River Runs Through It, All Right"

~ June 19 ~

"I am haunted by dogs." OK, so I'm no Norman Maclean. And unfortunately, if there's any river running through my life, it's a golden stream of dog pee. (I don't think Roomie realized how little bladder control pugs have when she brought Dog into our lives.)

You know that thing they say about fortune cookies, that whatever the fortune says, you should add "in bed" to the end of it? I feel like my life is like that now, except instead of "in bed" you can add the words "with dogs." (Yeah, 'cause there is definitely no "in bed" in my life right now! **sad face**) Suddenly, everywhere I go and everything I do and everyone one I meet has something to do with dogs. I seem to magnetically attract them. As if it isn't enough that I work at the frickin' Pup is Up, doggie headquarters of the United States.

For example: *Dines with Dogs*. This past weekend, Roomie and I go out for breakfast. Nothing fancy, just a simple walk down the street to grab a couple of bagels and a cup of coffee. We even leave Dog at home because dogs can't go into cafés, right? Wrong. When we get to the café, there's a whole line of people waiting to order at the counter, and every single one of them has a dog. Apparently, it's Dog's Day Out at the café. Fortune Cookie says: *You will have a chance encounter today (with dogs).*

Then there was yesterday, *Drives with Dogs*. It's a Saturday, and I've got errands to do. But Roomie has teacher-training all day at the school. I've got my keys in hand, and there's Dog, right by the front door, just waiting, practically begging to go with. He's still just a puppy and doesn't like to be left alone for long. Deep down, I'm really a softie (shhh!), and all I could think was, *Poor thing.* So I pick him up and take him with me, all over town. Me in the driver's seat and Dog with his ugly little face pressed in ecstasy against the passenger-side window (which he can barely reach), licking and slobbering the glass in sheer joy to be along for the ride. We went to the drive-up windows at the bank, the dry-cleaners, and the pharmacy. And then on the way home, we hit the drive-through beer carry-out. I had no idea there were so many drive-through businesses! Fortune Cookie says: *You will travel afar (with dogs).*

Works with Dogs, there's another. That was the day I took Dog to the office because the A/C was on the fritz at home. For once, I was glad I worked at The Pup is Up; I couldn't have gotten away with that anywhere else. Oh, and here's the kicker—you would not believe how many people came up to talk to me who had never given me the time of day before, including the Vice President of Sales. "Oh, I didn't know you had a dog!" "He's so cute!" "When did you get him?" "What a sweetie!" Who knows, maybe with all the extra attention I got, I'll finally get a promotion. Then my life could be Pay Raise with Dogs! Yeah, I'd be okay with that. Fortune Cookie says: *The harder you work, the luckier you get (with dogs).*

And of course, we come to the one I've been dreading, *Sleeps with Dogs*. Oh stop it. Not *that* kind of sleeping with, you pervert. Now this, as you can imagine, is not really my choice. It just inevitably happens that I wake up in the middle of the night and there's Dog in bed with me, hunkered down and completely immovable. I've stopped booting him out of the bed at this point; it's a losing battle. Kick him out, he comes right back. Put him outside the door, he whimpers until you let him back in. (Did I mention that I was a big ol' softie?) Stupid ugly dog. Stupid little ugly, lovable dog. What's a girl to do? Fortune Cookie says: *The secret to a happy life: accept what you cannot change (with dogs).*

16 ~ Tryst

~ July 6 ~

Noise reverberated off the walls as the Gaelic rock act onstage thundered through a fiddle-heavy number. Quasi-Irish wannabes stomped their feet and sucked down Guinnesses by the pint. Bodies were three-deep at the bar; getting a drink was next to impossible. Scowling, Mitch tried to weave his way closer, but he was wedged in. He let out a sigh of exasperation.

"Frustrating, isn't it?" a voice to his left cut through the din. He turned to find an attractive, petite blonde with a similar look of annoyance on her face. "What's a girl got to do to get a beer around here?"

"Darcy, is that you? Holy smokes!" He pushed his way through the crowd with a wide grin and enfolded the young lady in a huge bear hug. "I can't believe it! How are you?"

The blonde grinned. "Hey, Mitch. It's been forever."

"It has—too long! I guess we picked a bad night to come here," he shouted over the clamor. "I didn't know the Knockface Dollies were playing."

"Yeah, it's always a zoo when they're here," she agreed, exaggerating her words so he could hear her clearly.

"Hey, do you want to get out of here and find

somewhere a little less crazy? Maybe head down to Tryst, on the corner? It's not far; only a five-minute walk or so."

"Sure, let's go!"

*   *   *   *   *

"I've never been here," Darcy said, taking in the façade of the homely, clapboard building. The street lamp cast an alien glow over its aged wooden planks, where paint peeled off in flakes of dark, crusty brown.

"I'm not surprised. Most people probably think this place closed down years ago. There used to be a pink neon sign outside—looked like a little corner of Vegas, right here in Berlin Falls. It had a martini glass and a smoking cigarette, with a little curl of smoke that wrapped around the Y in 'Tryst.' I wonder what happened to that thing. It probably got busted up by a bunch of punks. Anyway, the sign's gone, so it can be kind of hard to find this place." He pulled on the rusty silver handle of the unmarked door. The door's small, round window was smoked over with a haze of grime. Darcy couldn't see a thing inside.

The bartender glanced over as Mitch entered the room. Without waiting for an order, he popped the top on a frosty bottle and slid it toward an empty bar stool at the end of the counter. Mitch claimed the seat and Darcy settled in next to him.

"You must be a regular here," Darcy deduced. He nodded, picking up the bottle to examine it. "I always take whatever's on special. I like surprises."

"Whatever floats your boat, I guess. Bartender, I'll have a vodka cran, please." The burly man behind the counter gave a curt nod and set to pouring.

Now that they were settled in a reasonably quiet place where they didn't have to shout to hear one another, they could finally talk. And Darcy could finally take a good look at how the years had treated her old friend. *Nice looking,* she thought. *I don't remember him being this cute. Huh.* She took note of his subdued jacket, his monochrome shirt and tie, his lack of flashy accessories or obvious money. *Nice features. Warm eyes, nice broad shoulders, soft-*

looking lips...a girl could definitely kiss this guy. She flirted with the idea for one brief moment. *No, not my type. Too bad.*

"Much better than MacDougal's, wouldn't you say?" Mitch ventured.

"Definitely. My ears were starting to ring in that place. I don't know why I go there anymore. Too many hipsters Instagramming with their iPhones. If they weren't so busy uploading pics of their 'awesome' lives, they might actually enjoy themselves."

Mitch laughed. "Right? So how've you been, anyway? I don't think we've seen each other since The Wherehouse closed."

"Good, really good! And I think you may be right." They reminisced for a while about the now-defunct art gallery, housed in a revamped warehouse in downtown Berlin Falls. The building had since been converted into a nightclub for the BDSM crowd, but once upon a time, both Mitch and Darcy had shown their work there. Mitch's exhibits primarily featured graphic illustrations he'd created as part of his college coursework requirements. Darcy's work was an entirely different animal. A self-trained artist, most of her inspiration came from "found" objects.

Mitch filled her in on his life since college: the graphic design job at The Pup is Up, where he lived now, and so on.

Her eyes lit up. "The Pup is Up? Cool! Which one? I shop at the one on Torrence Road all the time. I've got a labrador retriever named Sassafras."

"Nice. We do the graphic design work at headquarters, actually. I work on the advertising campaigns, signage for in-store promotions...stuff like that."

Darcy's course, on the other hand, had taken her well off the beaten path: a summer hiking the Appalachian trail, followed by several years in Europe, working as a nanny. "I just fell into that. Two years in Italy, one in France, and one in the UK."

"I'm surprised you came back here. It must seem pretty dull after Europe."

She shrugged. "I had a lot of good reasons to come back. I missed my family. And there's only so long one can be a nanny. I was just done with it. Anyway, Berlin Falls isn't so bad. It's affordable, especially compared to Europe, and there's a pretty good art scene here. I've even got my own little studio over in Vernon Village. I already had a lot of friends in the area, too, so it was kind of a no-brainer."

His beer was empty now. "Another drink?" he asked her. She nodded. He raised a finger in the air and twirled it, signaling the bartender for another round.

Mitch cast a sidelong glance at Darcy, seeing her again for the first time. Her stylish, shoulder-length haircut was a perfectly peroxided shade of platinum. Delicate features set off her sparkling blue eyes, and her upturned, pixie nose wrinkled adorably when she laughed. *Attractive*, he mused, *but not my kind of girl*. No ring on her finger, so he supposed she wasn't married. Two modest diamond studs winked from her earlobes. A pair of supple leather gloves in chocolate lay on the bar atop an exotic red clutch.

"So, are you seeing anyone?" he asked, already thinking of friends who might be interested in meeting her.

She made a face. "Nope. You?"

"No, not really. I kinda had this thing last month with my friend Kate, though. It was a real mess."

"This thing? Oh, you mean a hook-up. Yeah, hooking up with friends isn't usually the best idea. So do you like this girl?"

"She's a good friend, actually. That's what makes the situation so sticky."

"Maybe you should ask her out on a date," she suggested.

"A date? Ha! Kate doesn't date; she has kamikaze social outings with members of the opposite sex."

"That doesn't sound good."

"It's definitely not good. Kate's dreadful with men. She's been on more disastrous dates than anyone I know."

"Oh yeah?"

He chuckled, shaking his head. "Oh yeah. Let's see, first there was the former alcoholic who went on a bender.

Ooh, that was fun. I got to pick Kate up at a bar on campus because he wanted to keep drinking and she wanted to go home. Then, there was the over-aggressive salesman who set up a fake date with her to try to con her into joining his Ponzi scheme. Oh, and let's not forget the loony-toon who told her he loved her on the first date. Sometimes I think she dates these losers so that she doesn't have to really put her heart out there. You know, risk getting it broken. She got pretty badly dumped when we were in college. I'm not sure she ever got over the shock."

Darcy leaned back in her chair and studied him thoughtfully. "So you're not interested in her?"

"Even if I were, it's not gonna happen." He turned his head away to scan the room, not liking the turn this conversation had taken.

"Why not? You're good friends, and you've already slept together. That's usually the biggest hurdle."

"That was a mistake—just a one-time thing. Don't get me wrong. It was...nice..."

"Nice? Most guys I know would run screaming in the opposite direction from a girl they had 'nice' sex with. What are you saying, the sex wasn't good? Kate's too nice for you? What?" She rolled a finger around the lip of her wine glass, waiting for Mitch to explain himself.

Mitch clenched his jaw and glared into the distance at nothing, ignoring Darcy. A sideways glance crept her way, then retreated behind the stonewall again. He knocked back the rest of his beer and slammed the empty onto the bar with a sharp clack. "Damn, I need another drink!" He flagged down the bartender.

If he thinks I'm going to let the conversation drop, he's got another think coming. Darcy waited patiently, her arms crossed, one sandaled foot rocking lightly back and forth against the bronze foot rail. She'd obviously hit a sore spot, and one that needed to be examined.

Finally, he relented, realizing that his diversionary tactics weren't going to work. "I don't know what it is about Kate," he admitted in a low voice. "The night we had together was unlike anything I've ever experienced. And it wasn't about bells and whistles or mind-blowing bednastics. She just...loved me, that's all. I could *feel* it. It filled me up." He turned and met her eye in an unguarded moment. "I've never felt so happy before."

Darcy's heart went out to him. "How did you two end up, you know, *together*, anyway?"

Briefly, Mitch related the gruesome car accident that had unexpectedly claimed his father's life. "I was a zombie after he died. I got up every morning and went through the motions, but I wasn't really there. I don't remember much about those weeks, except that I didn't want to feel or think about anything. Then one day Kate showed up on my doorstep and wheedled her way in." Mitch recalled the image of Kate lovingly laying out dinner for the two of them, determined to get through to him somehow. "And she made me talk. Not unlike you're making me talk now," he grumbled, giving her a dirty look that said he was kind of grateful. "I'm not very good at talking about the big stuff, as you may have noticed."

"Yeah, I get that." She gave him a small smile of encouragement.

"Anyway, all those feelings I'd been pushing down hit the roof. It felt like I was going to throw up. And that's what I did, verbally anyway. I ended up blubbering like a baby. After a while, she tried to go, but...I asked her to stay." *Begged her to stay. Practically forced her to stay.* He leaned his head on one fist, a touch of guilt showing on his face. He couldn't help but wonder if he'd put Kate in an impossible position that night. *But she's the one who came to me. She's the one who knocked on my door. And she's the one who kissed me first...* "The rest, just happened." He let out a heavy sigh.

"Anyway, in the morning the alarm goes off like it does every day, and I hear this 'Oh shit!' from the other side of the bed. Next thing I know, she's shoving on her boots and racing for the door, saying she has to get home to change for work, and *poof*, she's gone."

"Wow. How are things between you now?" Darcy asked with a note of concern.

"Okay, I guess. Everything seems to have blown over, but it's still a little weird." Mitch and Kate had managed to get past the hook-up, at least on the surface of things. But in truth, that night had colored every minute they'd spent together since it happened.

"Maybe it's time for me to stop hanging out with Kate so much," he sighed. They'd been friends for so long that the idea was nearly unthinkable. He couldn't imagine a day without her.

Or maybe I'm in love. Crap.

17 ~ Gathering Wool

~ July 30 ~

Kate saw Mitch seated in one of the wooden booths on the other side of Donovan's and waved. As the weeks had passed, the two had found their way back to a more comfortable state of friendship. It was almost like their night together had never happened. Kate was glad, but she couldn't help feeling a wee bit of regret that things hadn't turned out another way instead. Every so often, she would find herself thinking of Mitch in ways that just weren't appropriate for mere friends, or even catch herself staring at him in a rather embarrassing manner. For the most part, she managed to rein in her mind, but she still had to remind herself on occasion to turn off those troublesome thoughts and switch over to the more mundane and acceptable feelings of being "just friends."

"Hey!" she greeted him, plopping down onto the cushy bench in a huff of relief. "How's your week been?"

"Good," he answered, sounding fairly cheerful. "Yours?"

"I can't complain. So, should we go for the usual?"

"Works for me." He flagged down the waitress. "Could we get the s'mores platter, please? And two Diet Cokes. Watching our figures, you know," he deadpanned, leaving the lumpy, somewhat sullen teen looking confused as to whether she should laugh politely or just walk away. She settled on a weak smile and trundled off to get their drinks.

"Chocolate for dinner, oh yeah. I'm so glad you're not some health nut. Then again, I'm pretty sure you like sweets even more than I do."

He grinned and tilted his head as if to say *touché*. "How well you know me, Kate." Her heart lurched with a brief flutter of emotion. She wondered if she would ever stop feeling that lurch when he looked at her with those warm, brown eyes of his. *Not if*, she commanded herself, *when*.

Kate filled up the silence before it could stretch out between them too meaningfully. "So how's work?"

They settled into a back-and-forth groove of the latest triumphs and tragedies they had each endured over the course of the last week. For Mitch, it was the never-ending saga of his officemate's power struggle with their boss.

Kate groaned in sympathy. "Ugh, that sucks. At least we don't have that kind of drama in the sales department. Everyone does their own thing all day, and the work is pretty cut-and-dried. Either you make your monthly sales goals or you don't, not much to argue about there. I guess it's different with you creatives. You know, I really envy you folks who can paint and draw and illustrate stuff on a computer—I'll never have that kind of creative talent. I love the stuff you do."

"Thanks," he said, smiling and holding her gaze for a moment.

Kate's heart skipped a beat at his genial smile. *Damnit, there I go again. He's just so darned cute.*

Their little almost-moment was mercifully interrupted by the waitress before it could become an actual moment. Gratefully, she skewered up a couple of marshmallows and prepped her graham crackers with a generous block of chocolate. She studied him out of the corner of one eye as he assembled his own chocolatey delights. *Maybe I should try again*, she thought, considering all that had happened between them since his father had passed. *Maybe things aren't quite so confusing for him anymore. Maybe he's ready for a bit more complication in his life. But how to approach the topic*...that was the trouble. She thought about it for a moment, then had an idea.

"So, the company banquet is coming up," she said. "Are you bringing anyone?" It was the one time of the year the company opened its purse strings and laid out a little cash for the enjoyment of its staff.

"Not likely."

Well shoot, that didn't tell me anything at all, she groused to herself. She supposed she'd have to be more direct.

"Oh, I just thought you might be seeing someone." There. She'd said it.

"Why would you think that?"

Kate felt a little sense of dread forming into a ball at the base of her throat. Maybe it hadn't been such a good idea to ask. But now that she had, she may as well push forward. "Well, you seem to be busier than usual lately, harder to get ahold of. I thought maybe..." she trailed off, leaving him to extrapolate the rest.

Mitch studied her with an evaluative gaze, as if trying to figure out what angle she was working from. Then he shrugged and said, "Nope. I joined a basketball league, that's all."

"Oh." Kate's mind flooded with relief. *Even if he's not interested in me anymore—if he ever was—at least there isn't someone else.* "I didn't know you played basketball."

"Last time I played was in high school. I'm pretty rusty, but it's been fun to play again. And it's been good to meet some new people. Some of the guys are pretty entertaining; we've been hanging out a bit. What about you?"

"What about me?" Kate asked, confused.

"Are you bringing anyone to the banquet?"

"Me? Heck no," she cracked. "Even if I were seeing someone, which I'm not," she thought she'd better add, "I wouldn't subject them to that kind of torture. What could be more boring than sitting through two hours of rubber chicken, corporate speeches, and watching people you don't know get awards for stuff you don't give a hoot about? 'And we'd like to welcome to the podium,' she mimicked, 'Marilyn MacFarland, winner of this year's Good Cheer award! Everybody give her a big hand now, why don't you?' Ugh."

"Ha! No doubt. Those endless awards and speeches make me want to hang myself from the rafters."

She laughed. "Maybe we should sit together, just in case. You know, do suicide watch for one another."

"Good idea. We can text each other smarmy comments to try to stave off the boredom."

"Deal!" she agreed, reaching across the table. Mitch's hand clasped onto hers and he gave it a firm squeeze. They both laughed easily as their arms lowered to rest on the table, his hand still holding hers. The tips of his fingers casually grazed down her palm, leaving a tingling trail wherever he touched. Kate felt the hair on her arms stand up. Mitch seemed entirely oblivious of his effect on her. Kate struggled to keep things light, when all she wanted to do was close her eyes and enjoy the feel of him touching her again.

Her mind drifted away. She imagined Mitch's fingers continuing up her arm, lightly scratching his fingernails over her tender skin. Then he was taking her by the hand and guiding her to the secluded hallway in the back of the restaurant...pinning her against the wood-paneled wall, pressing himself forward against her, lowering his head to give her a lingering kiss...

"Kate..." his voice broke through the gauzy layers of lust. She blinked, feeling his fingertips slipping away from hers one by one, his hand retreating across the table. Kate felt the mortification creeping up her neck; she needed to make a quick getaway.

"Excuse me for a minute, will you?" She fled from the table toward the back of the room. Seconds later she found herself safely in that same wood-paneled hallway, only this time, alone. She leaned against the wall in the spot where she had imagined the two of them entwined, about to kiss. Kate shook her head vigorously, then pushed through the door into the ladies room and splashed some cold water on her face. *Get a grip, girl!*

* * * * *

"Deal!" Kate reached across the table to grasp Mitch's hand. A rush of adrenaline coursed down his spine in a shudder. *Damn! Why does she still affect me this way?* Mitch struggled to maintain control despite the warning bells going off all throughout his body. His fingers roamed across her palm of their own accord; he couldn't seem to stop their movement. For just a second, Mitch indulged the fantasy. He daydreamed of pulling her closer to his side, sliding further into the booth and away from the prying eyes of others. Of kissing those sweet lips of hers for just as long as he wanted to, knowing that this time she wasn't going anywhere; she was exactly where she wanted to be...

"Kate," he murmured, the sound of his own voice awakening him from his tempting reverie. *Uh-oh.* He gently separated his fingers from hers and drew his hand away, discreetly reaching for his coat and dragging it across his lap. *If my pants could talk, they'd ask for the check. Good thing I don't have to stand up anytime soon,* he grimaced in discomfort. Across the table, he noted a deep scarlet blush spreading up Kate's neck toward her face. *Shit, I hope she's not a mind-reader.*

His fears were confirmed when she made a swift escape just seconds later. "Excuse me for a minute, will you?" she stuttered, practically running away from the table.

Idiot! Get ahold of yourself! But Mitch didn't know how to stop his overactive imagination. Hardly a day went by that he didn't think about the night he'd spent with Kate, the images replaying in his mind in exquisite torture.

It's hopeless! I'm a goner. Head over heels. In love. With Kate. Shit.

What the hell am I going to do now?

18 ~ Action Jackson

~ October 1 ~

Kate banged open the metal gymnasium door. Sweat-soaked heat smacked her in the face. She choked back her revulsion and stepped inside. The scuff of sneakers squeaked up and down the court as a tribe of tall urban warriors pounded over the glossy boards. Hair dripped with perspiration, and saturated shirts clung to well-muscled chests and beer-guts alike.

Kate made her way to the fold-out bleachers at one end of the court, scanning the floor for Mitch. The weeks had continued to pass, and more and more, their night together faded, losing its sharp edges. They had settled back into the familiar routine of chats in the hallway at work and weekly dinners out, where they caught up on news and avoided discussion of anything terribly deep. If there had been a window of opportunity for anything more between them, it seemed to have passed once again.

A tangle of bodies grappled at mid-court, pinballing off one another in testosterone-charged attempts to secure the ball. She rolled her eyes and grabbed a seat a couple of rows up, pulling out her smart phone to while away the time with a quick game of Words With Friends. *Damn, these letters suck! Why do I always get the Q and the X at the same time?* Kate grumbled to herself. But before she could reply (and wonder whether she was slightly insane for having a conversation with herself)...*SMACK!*

"Oww!" The basketball bounced back down onto the court, having struck her square on the forehead. A pair of well-worn high-tops rushed into Kate's swimming field of vision.

"Oh my gosh, I'm so sorry!" she heard a voice stammer. She cradled her throbbing temple in one hand and wiped away tears of surprised pain with the other. Slowly, her eyes made their way up from the man's shoes—a *long* way up; dang, this guy was tall!—until they reached his red-stained, panting face. Somewhere in the background, a whistle shrilled, and players drifted off the court as the scrimmage ended.

The sweaty man took a seat on the bleacher in front of Kate, at eye level with her now. Concern showed in his storm-grey eyes—*nice eyes*, she couldn't help but notice. *A lot of nice things, actually*, she mused as she sized up his muscular bare arms, incredibly large hands, and Dudley Do-Right chin. A bead of sweat traced down his neck past his wildly pulsing carotid, slipping down through the fine mat of hair that curled up from beneath his jersey. Kate's throat went dry, and she sucked in her lower lip, chewing on it for half a second before catching herself and rearranging her features into a more seemly countenance.

*   *   *   *   *

JP could see in an instant that the woman he'd smacked in the face didn't belong here. Business casual pants, peachy-colored blouse, leather satchel—no doubt stuffed full of *New York Times* best sellers and Doublemint chewing gum—and a complete lack of interest in what was happening on the court. He'd noticed her as she entered the gym and found a seat. *Attractive. No, strike that—very attractive.* He took in her wavy, brown hair, its long strands neatly brushed back away from her pretty face, and her lush figure—especially her ample bosom. *What a rack!*

Easy enough to get her attention, he'd thought. Just send an errant ball her way, make eye contact, and *voilà*, the rest would be history. It usually was with women, and he saw no reason why this particular woman would be any different. Unfortunately, he miscalculated and sent the ball flying right into her face instead of the harmless ricochet off the bleachers he'd intended.

He jogged up to the bleachers at a sprint, where the woman sat cradling her head in her hands and swearing. *Minus one*, he made a mental note. *A woman swearing? That's just plain unattractive. Already, this girl's stock is going down.* But then she turned her face up toward him and he got a good look down the front of her clingy blouse. He came to a halt and spluttered an apology, all the while trying not to stare at those marvelous, fleshy breasts beneath that peachy silk. She must not have realized that one more button was open than she had probably intended. He suppressed a grin of appreciation and sat down just below her, where he wouldn't be tempted to look down her shirt again. *Okay, plus one; we're back to even. I've got nothing else going on at the moment, anyway. I could use a good banging if I can get one...and I certainly could do worse than banging those fabulous knockers.*

* * * * *

She noticed his grey eyes drop for just a moment. She could've sworn he was trying to look down her shirt, but the moment passed before she could be sure. Still in a daze, she allowed the man to take her hand. He cupped it between his palms and squeezed earnestly. The heat from his hands shot up her arm and spread throughout her body in an electric surge. Her whole body tuned into him instantly. *I suppose it might be frowned upon if I were to slam this man up against the wall and take advantage of him here and now.* Slightly appalled at herself (after all, he was a big, sweaty jock—just the kind of guy she *didn't* need to get involved with), she removed her hand from his and rubbed it across her forehead. He seemed to be apologizing, if she could just focus on his words. She found herself wondering about the size of those hands of his, and whether the old adage really held true.

"I don't know how that ball got away from me. Really, are you okay? Are you hurt?" Kate realized that she hadn't uttered a word to confirm that she was, in fact, all right.

"Yes, yes," she said, somewhat grumpily. "I'm fine. Or rather, I'll be fine in a few minutes, I'm sure." She tried to flash a polite smile, the best she could manage between her pounding head and her knocking knees. She shifted in her seat uncomfortably. *This is ridiculous. One whiff of this guy's über-jock pheromones and I'm swooning like a milkmaid in some pastoral poem.* She knew it was all hormonal, but somehow, that kind of logic didn't make the overwhelming randiness she felt in this gorgeous hunk's presence go away.

"Kate!" a familiar voice cut through her thoughts. Mitch came bounding up with a huff and plopped down on the bench in front of her. "Are you okay?" He cast a veiled glance over at JP, trying his best to hide his annoyance and alarm. The tall man sat at Kate's feet, his eyes drinking her in like a highball glass of single malt at the end of a long day at work. *Damnit, this is NOT what I needed. Just when things are getting back to normal with Kate, in comes this manwhore!* It just wasn't fair. Mitch could tell by the stupefied look on Kate's face that it was too late. She was already hooked. Well, he would still do what he could to get her away from him, and fast.

"Come on, Kate, let's get you home. We can order in instead of going out. Catch you later, JP." Even though it wasn't technically true, it wouldn't hurt to let JP think that he was taking Kate out on a date. They did have plans to go out to dinner—but only as friends, like always. *Still, JP doesn't know that.* Kate nodded absently and started to get up. But before Mitch could spirit her away, JP jumped up and reclaimed her hand.

"Oh, no, let me! Dinner is the least I could do after whacking you on the head like that. Really, I feel awful." He could see Kate teetering on the edge of indecision, and pounced on the opportunity. "Yes," he barreled forward confidently, helping her step down from the bleachers, "a little homemade comfort food, and you'll feel better in no time. I know just the place." JP turned and began to lead her toward the exit, stopping to grab his windbreaker from a nearby bench. "You coming, Shorty? We can catch up on old times," he tossed back at Mitch. Not that he had any intention of letting Mitch come along for the ride. "Mitch and I went to high school together," he explained to Kate.

Mitch bristled. He was not short! He was six-foot-one. He just wasn't gargantuan, like this incredible meathead. Swallowing his ire, he plastered a smile on his face in that "I can take a joke" kind of way, and answered back, "You bet. I just need to get my things from the locker room. I'll meet you outside, Kate." She nodded faintly as JP whisked her off to the door. Mitch had a feeling it was going to be a long night.

That feeling of irritation changed to one of gloom when he pushed out through the doors of the gymnasium to find Kate gone. Rain pounded down around him. *Damnit, I should have known!* he cursed, sticking the keys into the door of his Pontiac and yanking it open. *Crap, I don't know where they went, either.* He yanked out his phone and shot off a text to Kate, then got in the car and waited.

And waited. Five minutes, no response. He texted Kate again. He lowered his head onto his arms, burying his face in the steering wheel. Then the response came.

"Rain check?"

His shoulders sagged glumly, and he started up the engine for the solitary drive home.

*   *   *   *   *

They stepped out into a chilly September drizzle. Kate pulled her coat around her, not quite ready to embrace the inevitably unpleasant weather of fall. This was just the beginning of what would be many months of cold, dark, and nasty weather, thanks to Berlin Falls' northern clime. She shrank back into the protective overhang of the gymnasium door, loath to step out into the rain.

JP touched her elbow lightly. "Let me get my car," he

offered, hustling out into the rain before she could protest. Moments later, he pulled up in his gently battered Jeep and popped open the passenger door from the inside. "Hop in!"

Kate looked uncertain. "I was waiting for Mitch..."

"Mitch can meet us at the diner. Come on!" he urged. Kate glanced behind her at the metal door, then shrugged and clambered into JP's car.

"Well, okay, I guess," Kate relented. Considering how awkward things had been with Mitch in the last few months, she wasn't sure she wanted him along on this one, anyway. Not when there was a smoking hot man sitting next to her who she was rather intrigued to get to know. *I'll just reschedule with Mitch. He won't mind; we see each other every day at work anyway.*

*   *   *   *   *

"Hmm, cozy," Kate remarked skeptically, scanning the run-down, garishly lit room as they stepped through the door of The Working Man. A handful of customers dotted the joint: a man at the counter reading a newspaper over a cup of coffee, an older couple sitting on the same side of a booth and leaning into one another, a passel of students hoovering grilled cheese sandwiches and milkshakes. The usual suspects at a mom-and-pop diner, Kate supposed.

"Give it a chance," JP said in a lighthearted tone of voice. "The food is really good. And besides, I know the owners." He winked as he ushered her to a booth near the clunky old jukebox. A tune that sounded vaguely fifty years ago wheezed out of its internal organs, barely parting the air with its rusty notes.

"If you say so," Kate smiled brightly, sinking into the red vinyl cushioning of the booth with a squeak. JP sat down across from her, quietly folding his hands in his lap. He leaned back comfortably, wearing that confident demi-smile of his, as if he were Mona Lisa's brother in the flesh. It unnerved her. Her eyes fluttered as she cast her gaze down at the menu, studying it with intense interest to cover her flustered state. Now that they were here, sitting face to face, she had no idea what to say to this undeniably hunky man.

She glanced up to find both JP and the waitress staring at her. "Ahem," piped the matronly woman in beige flats and a lace-collared gingham dress in a faded shade of carnation. Unnaturally dark support hose had started to scrunch downward toward the woman's cankles. A bounty of silver-grey curls looped about her head—those huge curls that you only get from those enormous, prickly, plastic curlers like your grandmother used to use to set your hair when you were eight years old. Kate wondered how long it must've taken this woman to arrange her coif into such perfect O's of elderliness.

"So what'll it be?" the waitress asked—again apparently, Kate gathered from her acerbic tone. Kate quickly mumbled something about club sandwiches and pickles. *Pickles, really? I hate pickles. Ugh.*

*   *   *   *   *

Grease oozed into the paper napkins that cushioned the basket of fried pickles. Kate's stomach turned. She discreetly pushed them aside and concentrated on attacking the mile-high sandwich falling apart all over her plate. It was a total mess and an eyesore, but it was, as promised, tasty.

So far they'd covered the usual topics: the whole what-do-you-do-for-a-living-where-do-you-live-oh-you-must-know-so-and-so-who-lives-just-down-the-street, and so on. They had a few things in common, somewhat to Kate's surprise. He had a degree in history (her minor in college) and was an avid fan of classic sci-fi literature.

"...*Prelude to Foundation* was clearly the best of the bunch," JP expounded, referring to Isaac Asimov's *Foundation* series of books. "It's the best written, and it's got the most action, not to mention all the incredible ideas he comes up with. The sheer amount of detail is mind-blowing."

"You're smoking crack! *Foundation's Edge* is way better. There may not be as much action, but the characters are incredible. I couldn't put it down. The story is good enough to stand on its own, and you can't say that about the other books in the series."

JP threw his hands up. "To each his own. I guess we'll just have to agree to disagree."

She grinned and decided to let that one pass. It was only their first date—if this could be considered a date. There would be time later to make him see the error of his ways. "So tell me about this yoga retreat you went on. Costa Rica, was it?" she asked, tucking into the second half of her gloppy sandwich.

"Yeah. I just got back about two weeks ago. It was so relaxing. It's really hard to come back to reality after something like that. We had sunrise yoga sessions every morning, guided meditations in the afternoon, breathwork, inversions workshops, you name it. And the food was amazing. Everything fresh and local. All vegetarian of course."

"Really?" She eyed his plate of chicken fried steak, and he chuckled.

"Hey, I can't be good all the time. I'll go back to wheatgrass and tofu tomorrow."

"I never would've pegged you as a yoga guy. Let me guess—you got into it for the hot, bendy women, right?"

JP threw his head back and hooted. "Well you got me there. I can't deny the ladies were part of the appeal. I do appreciate a fine feminine figure," he confessed, casting an eye suggestively over Kate's voluptuous frame. He paused to be sure she took his intent. Her eyes widened and she couldn't suppress a little grin.

"But in all seriousness," he continued, "it was my high school coach that got me into yoga in the first place. He was nearly sixty and still as limber as a rag. He swore up and down that yoga was his secret weapon. We did ten or fifteen minutes every day as part of our warm-ups at practice."

"Somehow, I can't imagine Mitch doing yoga," she grinned. "What was he like in high school, anyway?"

"Probably about the same as he is now. At least, he doesn't seem very different from then. We haven't really spent much time hanging out since league started. He was a good guy in high school, and a decent shot on the court. Quiet, though. I guess that hasn't changed. I don't think he liked me much in high school, but I could never figure out why. Anyhow, that's all water under the bridge—ancient history."

The waitress reappeared to clear the table. Kate glanced down to find her plate cleared and the basket of fried pickle chips nearly empty. A tiny burp rumbled up from deep within her gut, which gurgled with displeasure. Thankfully, neither JP nor the blue-hair seemed to notice, as they were deep in conversation of their own.

"No, it just hasn't been the same since Frank retired. I hear ya, Erma," JP was saying to the pudgy woman.

"Darn right. I don't know why he had to go and move to Florida anyway. He probably joined some nudist club with a bunch of other old folks. That sounds exactly like something Frank would do, mmm-mmm," Erma clucked in disapproval. "Who wants to see a bunch of old, saggy people naked anyway? Not me, that's for sure."

Kate joined with JP in a hearty laugh at the idea of this unknown Frank character sunning his wrinkled buns poolside at some shabby resort long past its 1970s heyday. "And Frank is...?" she asked.

"The previous owner of this charming little joint," JP replied. "And my great-uncle. We've been coming to this place ever since I was a kid. Erma here used to babysit for me and my brother Rudy until I hit eighth grade or so. Rudy and I both worked here all through high school. I've probably eaten my weight in meatloaf sandwiches here a hundred times over."

"A hundred?" snorted Erma. "Try a thousand!"

Kate grinned at their easy repartee. They were practically family. Guess that would explain why JP still frequented the place, even though there were plenty of nicer diners around town. "So who's back in the kitchen?" she asked. "Your mother?"

JP's eyes crinkled with laughter. "Well actually, now that you mention it..." He winked. And not just because he was kidding.

*　　*　　*　　*　　*

Kate closed the front door behind her and slung her purse over a hook on the coat rack, glad to be back to her own little safe zone. JP was the last thing she'd been expecting to cross her radar, and even though the prospect of a new man in her life was exciting, she was still feeling a bit unprepared for this sudden dive back into the dating pool. She peeked out the window, shifting the curtain to one side slightly to view the curb. JP's car had already pulled away.

She pivoted to find herself face to face with Evette. She started. "Geez, woman! You and your sneaky feet." She took in Evette's garb as her heartbeat slowed back to normal. A fluffy lilac robe draped down past her ankles, and her perfectly painted toenails peeped out from feathered, high-heeled house slippers in white. A matching white towel neatly hid her black curls in a downy swirl atop her head.

"What, no face mask?" Kate snarked, reaching out to pet Drama, who was cradled under his mama's right arm.

"Cucumber mask is next!" Evette chirped. "So where've you been that's got you looking so stirred up?"

How does she always seem to know?! It was annoying, but also part of the fun of living with her best friend. Kate figured she may as well dive in, since hiding anything from Evette never seemed to work. "I met a new guy." She waggled her eyebrows with a huge grin.

"Ooh la la! Do tell!" Evette grabbed her wrist and pulled her toward the bathroom, where her nightly beauty routine was underway. "I had a feeling—I couldn't help but notice the strange car in front of the house. You guys sure were out there for a while..." she hinted.

Kate snorted. "Yeah, I barely managed to escape before he pawed my clothes off. He certainly doesn't make any bones about what he wants from me. No pun intended."

Kate was expecting a laugh, but instead, Evette's face fell. "Oh. Another dud, eh?"

"It was kind of refreshing, actually. It's nice to know

exactly what a man wants for a change."

"Even if what this guy wants is just sex?"

"Maybe. Uncomplicated sex with no strings and no history to worry about? It's pretty tempting at the moment. And if JP's as good in bed as he is at kissing, it could be one hell of a ride."

"But you didn't invite him in," Evette observed, smearing on a heavy dollop of yogurt-cucumber glop.

"Naw. I just met him tonight. He's going to have to work for it a bit harder than that. Boy, was he surprised, though. I could tell by the look on his face when I got out of the car. He obviously thought he had it in the bag." She grabbed her toothbrush out of the medicine cabinet and bumped Evette over with one hip.

"Weren't you supposed to be going to dinner with Mitch tonight?"

Kate's mouth twisted as she squeezed out some toothpaste. "Yes." She knew Evette wouldn't like it, but she may as well tell the whole truth. "I asked for a rain check." She stuck the toothbrush in her mouth and started brushing vigorously.

"You what? Oh for Pete's sake, Kate. Blowing off Mitch for some hot-and-ready Freddy? Stay classy, girl." Evette gave her a dirty look in the bathroom mirror as she picked up her tweezers and began to attack her eyebrows. Drama yipped, sensing her displeasure, and pushed between their legs to rear up on the cabinet.

Kate's anger surged. She spit into the sink and returned Evette's dirty look times three. "Screw you, Vetta. Not everyone has sworn off men because of one bad egg, you know. You may be convinced that Mitch and I are a match made in heaven, but things don't seem to be turning out that way, do they? It's been four months, and nothing has changed. He's the one who said we should just be friends, and he's never said anything different. I'm just taking him at his word. If we're 'just friends,' then he'd better get used to me dating other guys."

She let out a sigh of frustration. This constant speculation about Mitch and where their relationship stood was exhausting. The mixed signals he sent her way were absolutely maddening. Some days, he was solicitous, warm, and affectionate. Other days, he was cold and distant, too reserved to reach. Kate still didn't know how she felt about Mitch, and she was even less sure how he felt about her.

Evette's face softened, and she placed a manicured hand on Kate's shoulder. "I still think you're giving up too easily. Mitch is a great guy."

"Yes, I know. He's super." *Handsome. Sweet. Good in bed...* "There's just so much baggage between us now. And besides, actions speak louder than words. What actions have I got to go on from Mitch lately? Zero. He's hardly even given me a hug in the last four months, much less tried to kiss me."

"Maybe he's afraid to get too close," Evette said pointedly. "You didn't exactly handle the whole situation very well, so far as I can tell."

Evette's words stung. *The truth always does*, she thought. Her roommate had a point. She still kicked herself sometimes for her thoughtless behavior in the days after she and Mitch had slept together. *He probably thinks I'm a praying mantis, ready to bite his head off and chew it up after mating.*

Her emotional high from flirting with JP all evening was starting to wear off; she wasn't ready to let it go just yet. "Be that as it may, it's water under the bridge now. I've got a new guy who's made his interest in me crystal clear, and you know what? I'm tired of being single. So if I decide to give JP a chance, that's my business. Maybe he's just a horndog, and all he has to offer is a good roll in the hay. But why not? He's sexy as hell, and I don't see anything wrong with enjoying a man's company. What can I say, a hard man is good to find!" She smirked at her borrowed witticism—one of her favorite quotes from Mae West.

Evette finished rubbing the gooey mask off her face. "Yeah, 'cause a roll in the hay got you so far with Mitch."

Kate glared at her friend in the mirror. "That was low, Vetta. Really low."

Evette draped her arms over Kate's shoulders, hugging

her from behind and resting her chin on Kate's shoulder. She met her friend's furious eyes in the mirror. "I'm sorry, hon. You're right. I apologize." She hesitated, but being Evette, she always had to say the full 100% of what was on her mind. "But don't you want something deeper? A meaningful love connection?"

Kate sniffed, her eyes softening. "Sure, I do. But it doesn't seem like that's going to happen with Mitch, and I need to move on. Move forward. Just move! I won't whitewash it here; I need some action. And *voilà*, Action Jackson falls right into my lap. Is he the kind of guy I want to marry? Probably not. Do we have a lot in common, similar goals in life? Who knows. I'm not sizing him up for his witty conversation or brilliant personality. Why should guys be the only ones who get to scratch that itch?" Kate scooped up Drama from the tiled floor and stalked back out to the living room, leaving Evette in a state of slack-jawed speechlessness. She flopped down on the couch and turned on the boob tube, flipping the channels distract-edly, settling on a marathon of *Firefly* reruns.

Kate couldn't help but wonder if Mitch was sweating her defection to JP this evening. *Well, if he's jealous, it's nobody's fault but his own. If he wanted to be with me, he's had plenty of chances to step up to the plate and give it another crack. But he hasn't. Action Jackson, one. Captain Conservative, zero.*

And besides, it was fall now, and nothing was more fun than being part of a couple in the fall. With JP by her side, Kate could enjoy all those seasonal "coupley" things that she loved to do so much. They could goof around in the corn mazes at the local apple farm. Buy hot chocolate. Stroll hand in hand "oohing" and "ahhing" at the autumn leaves. Even sitting on the couch and swearing at football games would be pretty darned fabulous compared to being alone—and lonely. Maybe she and JP wouldn't be the ideal couple, but it would be nice just to be with someone. To have a special companion to do things with. And yes, oh yes—to get laid. Absolutely to get laid.

19 ~ A FULL BELLY AND AN EMPTY COCK

~ October 6 ~

Her second date with JP would begin in just an hour. Kate lay back in the frothy bathwater, twirling a hand through the warm bubbles, considering their interactions thus far.

At the gym, where he'd ricocheted a basketball off her head. A less-than-awesome way to start things off, but bonus points for the sweaty pheromones.

Then at The Working Man. Kind of a dump, but she supposed it did have personality. Still, the built-up grunge in the corners of the linoleum floor was so old that there were probably fossilized trilobites in there. She wrinkled her nose. *I guess the Queasy Spoons of the world are just not for me.*

Then there was JP's rather beat-up Jeep. Jerseys and sneakers were heaped on the back seat. Crumbs, gum wrappers, crumbling leaves, and old parking tickets littered the oil-stained carpet pads in the front. The car obviously hadn't been cleaned for at least a few weeks. *Yuck.* She dreaded to think what his house looked like, especially knowing he shared a bathroom with three other guys.

Kate wondered what he had up his sleeve for the

evening. He'd played it cool when she'd asked about their plans. All he would say is, "You'll like it, trust me," words which never failed to arouse her inner skeptic. What clichéd trick from the Dating 101 book would he throw her way to try to impress her? The live-jazz date, to show that he was more than just a jock? The classic dinner-and-a-movie, which he would insist on paying for, thus making her feel guilty if she opted out of tonsil hockey at the end of the evening? Or perhaps he'd be off the mark entirely, taking her to a sports bar to watch ten screens' worth of games she didn't give a rat's ass about. Briefly, she wondered if she should just invite him into her apartment straight off and skip all that unnecessary hoopla, but quickly vetoed the idea. She didn't know him well enough yet to be inviting him in for the night.

She stepped out of the bath and patted herself down with an oversized, seafoam-green bath towel. *Damn, I forgot to shave. Oh well, one more reason not to get naked tonight.* She padded down the hallway to her bedroom and slipped inside, closing the door behind her. *What to wear, what to wear.* Since she didn't know where they were going, she decided to dress for comfort rather than style. Based on his enthusiastic pursuit of her thus far, Kate could be pretty certain JP was a sure thing, so she didn't feel the need to go to great lengths to impress him. Still, that didn't mean she planned to dress like a slob. She liked looking stylish as much as the next girl—*though perhaps not as much as Evette. One good thing about having a clothes-horse for a roommate—she always has great clothes to borrow!*

Kate pulled out pair of True Religion bootcut jeans to go with Evette's Vivienne Tam wrap blouse in teal. She slipped into the outfit and checked her figure in the cheval glass that stood in the corner of her room, nodding with satisfaction. A pair of high-heeled boots, a bit of glitter dust in the décolletage, a pair of pear drop earrings, and *voilà*. The perfect second-date outfit. Not too dressy, and not too much jewelry; clothes just nice enough to upgrade to a nicer restaurant if that's where the evening led.

She twisted her hair back into a no-fuss knot and

secured it with a pair of vintage hair sticks, each one topped with an art-deco swirl of pearls and rhinestones. Kate wasn't much of a girly-girl, but she did have a weakness for vintage jewelry—especially vintage hair accessories. A few swipes of blush, a little mascara (brown, never black), and a light touch of tinted lip gloss finished the look. She stepped back to evaluate the final product and gave herself a passing grade. *At least an A-minus. Good enough for a second date, anyway.* After one last glance in the mirror to tuck back a stray hair, Kate adjourned to the kitchen to mix herself a quick Pimm's cup in anticipation of JP's arrival. *All systems go!*

* * * * *

The door reverberated with an assertive knock. *No doubt who that is.* Kate opened the door to find JP, looking surprisingly dapper. Pressed black slacks, spotless. Broadcloth shirt in deep crimson, very smart. Casual jacket in dark heather grey, classic. Hair neatly combed back, face freshly shaven. An alluring waft of cologne filled her nostrils as JP pressed a gentlemanly kiss on Kate's cheek. "Good evening," he said warmly, a genial sparkle in his eyes.

"Wow, look at you!" Kate spluttered, somewhere on the verge of astonishment. "You look fantastic!" So much for the cool reserve she'd been planning to keep up throughout the evening.

"I clean up all right," he joked, stepping aside as she exited the house. "You're looking lovely yourself. Ready to go?" She murmured a demure thanks and nodded. He escorted her to the car and opened the passenger door for her, taking her hand to help her into the vehicle. Kate was amazed at the transformation that had taken place. Gone were the wadded-up sweat pants and the tumble of untied sneakers. Every last crumb and piece of trash had been removed and the carpet was freshly shampooed. The dashboard shone with a recent coat of gloss. It even smelled fresh inside, with a new scented doodad hanging from the rearview mirror. Kate was impressed. It gave her hope that perhaps JP wasn't a total slob after all.

He cranked the motor and away they went. "So where are we going?" Kate asked. "Downtown?"

"Never you mind," he teased. "I've got just the spot!"

After a few minutes of small talk, JP pulled the car into the parking lot of a place Kate knew well: the Bright Harvest Market. This indoor farmers' market was one of the city's most popular destinations for food, drink, and serious cheese, both local and imported. It was one of Kate's favorite destinations in Berlin Falls.

"Oooh, perfect! I love this place."

A gratified smile spread over JP's face. "I thought you might. You seem like a gal who appreciates good food."

"You know me pretty well for someone who barely knows me," she kidded. "They say the way to a man's heart is through his stomach, but I'm pretty sure they actually wrote that about me."

"I don't know how I ever guessed. Could be the way you attacked that basket of fried pickles at the diner. Fried pickles, really?"

She burst out laughing. "I don't know what I was thinking. My stomach hurt for the rest of the night after eating those."

"Guess that's why I didn't get invited in..."

"Ha ha. Don't get ahead of yourself, Casanova," she gave him a playful push as they made their way toward the entrance.

"Oh, I don't need to get ahead of myself," he fired back. "I only need to get ahead of you."

She shook her head and grinned at his audacity. *"Touché."*

He offered the crook of his arm with a debonair eyebrow raised. She inclined her head and accepted, lacing her hands around his upper arm. *Mmmm, firm biceps...* She smiled secretly at the thought that perhaps soon, he'd be wrapping those iron arms of his around her.

As they entered the vast hall, Kate stopped in her tracks and looked around in wonder. The market was fully decked out for autumn. Stacks of hay bales showcased jugs of cider, baskets of harvest fruits, and vibrant potted mums in white, yellow, orange, red, and purple. Pumpkins and gourds were piled knee-deep at the foot of golden sheaves of corn and sunflowers. Displays of homemade brittle, jams and jellies, and raw local honey beckoned to those with a sweet tooth. It was hog heaven for foodies.

Kate rummaged through her leather bag and pulled out a small digital camera. "Let's take some pics," she suggested. They ambled up and down the crowded aisles of the market, taking turns snapping photos and pointing out picture-worthy vignettes: bundles of lavender tied with twine; glass-encased piles of marzipan, Bavarian cookies, and hand-dipped chocolates; the classic "happy family" (L.L.Bean-clad mom, dad, and ruddy-cheeked lad) bellied up to the counter of the Vietnamese noodle joint, slurping down hot bowls of pho to combat the chill outside; the cellophane-wrapped bouquets finished with evergreen branches and pine cones; and all manner of people passing by in an endless parade. Along the way, Kate and JP picked up the makings for a picnic dinner.

They found a small table in the dining area and spread out their purchases. JP groaned at the sheer volume of goodies. "You think maybe we went overboard?"

"Nah!" Kate exclaimed. "We're just doing our part to support local merchants, right? Dig in!" She tore off a hunk of still-warm peasant bread, slathered it with hand-churned butter, and topped it with tranches of grilled eggplant, sliced fontina, and sundried tomatoes swimming in olive oil and herbs. "Mmmm," she moaned with pleasure as she bit into the gastronomical creation. "Foodgasm."

JP's eyes widened in amusement, but his mouth was too full of cream-cheese stuffed kalamatas to comment. Several minutes of heavenly eating ensued; conversation dropped off to an appreciative "ooooh" here and a "here, try this" there. Spicy cilantro hummus and grilled pita, onion confit, mini crab cakes, carpaccio with shaved parmesan and capers, toasted ravioli bites with vodka sauce...each morsel was more scrumptious than the last.

"Seriously, too much!" JP assessed the food remaining on the table while rubbing his distended stomach. "What were we thinking?"

"We were thinking it would be delicious, and we were right!" Kate sighed in contentment. "We should wrap the leftovers up and take them home. That's some world-class midnight snacking, there." She joked lightly, leaning forward to rest her head on one elbow on the table.

"Or we could have it for breakfast." JP leaned in close to face off against her, his grey eyes smoldering with interest.

This guy's about as subtle as a baseball bat to the forehead. Be that as it may, she was willing to overlook it in this case. *This is a man who knows what he wants when he sees it, and goes after it.* She had no doubt he would be delightfully aggressive in bed, too. In her mind, he was already tumbling her in the sheets, pinning her down with his sleek body...

If only Mitch could be so straightforward with his wants and desires. She couldn't prevent the thought from springing up, effectively squelching the cozy-hot fantasy of herself and JP. *But Mitch can't do that. Nope, I'd much rather be with a guy like JP*, she mused, summing him up in a few broad swipes. *This is a man with simple needs: a full belly and an empty cock. Yep, that sounds like just my speed right now. Someone whose wants and needs are easy to read and probably just as easy to fulfill.*

Pulling her focus back to the man leaning over the table toward her, she smiled slowly and with meaning, reaching out to lightly run her hand up his arm, wrapping it around his elbow and giving a gentle tug in her direction—just enough pressure to let him know that if he wanted to get even closer to her, now would be a good time. Without waiting for further invitation, he closed the distance between them and brushed a tantalizing kiss across her lips, lingering for a few moments, sweeping his mouth across hers, barely touching.

Kate's toes tingled and her blood began to sing. It wasn't what she had been expecting, but it was all the more scintillating for that. Once again, she found herself realizing that JP was a man full of surprises. *There may be more to this one than meets the eye.* Any further thoughts were chased away as JP pulled her closer for a more thorough introduction of the kissing variety. The date was going much better than she had anticipated, indeed.

20 ~ FALL DOWN SEVEN TIMES

~ October 10 ~

Mitch stepped out of the car and waved to Darcy, who was leaning on the brick wall next to the parking lot.

"Have any trouble finding the place?" she asked.

"Nope, pretty easy." He gave her a quick hug.

"It used to be an elementary school, believe it or not." From the utilitarian look of the brick building, Mitch could believe it. Blocks of rectangular windows covered every wall, and a set of ugly concrete steps led up to the metal double-doors that formed the main entrance.

"The rooms are hideous, but they're great for art studios. The linoleum floors are a snap to clean, and the light is fantastic. On the other hand, the pint-size toilets and kid-height sinks, not so fantastic," Darcy grinned. "My room's on the second floor. Come on."

They entered the building and tramped up the mint-green stairwell to the second floor. Darcy fished out a key on a yellow lanyard from her bag and jimmied open the door of her studio after several tries. "Sorry, the door likes to stick. Come on in."

She flipped on the light switch as they stepped inside. A large easel with an unfinished portrait of a young woman dominated the center of the room. To one side, a paint-splattered wooden table was buried beneath tubes of acrylic paint, plastic cups full of brushes, and cardboard boxes stuffed with miscellaneous supplies. A second table was home to a small etching press. Clusters of prints framed in thick, white matboard leaned against the walls around the room, and one tall bookshelf was crammed with salvaged items that some would undoubtedly call "junk."

"I love what you've done with the place," Mitch teased. Darcy rolled her eyes at him. He walked over to examine some of the objects on the bookshelf: twisted wires, scraps of fabric, buttons, jar lids, seashells, beads, oddly shaped twigs, and even a toy squirt gun. "What are you going to do with all this stuff?"

"I'm thinking about making a series of sea creatures. Angel fish, seahorses, that kind of thing. I plan to make a base for each piece out of upcycled wood blocks and wire."

Darcy gave him a lengthy tour around the room, explaining various works-in-progress and rifling through the collection of prints to look for specific pieces to show him. "These prints have been stacking up lately, since I've been experimenting with the new press. I sell a good number of them every month at the Open House, though. Helps to pay the rent on this place. I've mostly been working with proverbs lately." She handed him a black-and-white print, accented with handpainted strokes in delicate watercolors. "Fall down seven times, stand up eight," it read. The picture showed a newborn foal, struggling to stand on spindly legs.

Mitch breathed in the smells of the room as he carefully returned the print to its place. "Being here really makes me miss my days in the studio," he said wistfully, tucking his hands into the pockets of his jeans and rocking back and forth from heel to toe.

Darcy snorted. "I'll trade you a steady income for all the studio time you want. It seems like I'm here 24-7 anymore, and with not much to show for it. Here," she handed him a small cardboard box full of bottle caps. "Sort these by color, would you?" She took up a small brush and began adding detailed strokes to the portrait of the young woman.

"What would you think about me coming over every so often to do some artwork of my own? I'd be happy to chip in a bit on the studio."

"That's not a bad idea," Darcy nodded thoughtfully, staring at the canvas. "I've been cooped up in here so much lately, it might be good to have some company. Let me think about it, okay?"

"Sure." Mitch set the box down and started picking through it, plucking out various colored caps and sorting them into piles. "You know, anytime you need a break, just give me a call. You should come out with Kate and me. We have dinner almost every week, and I think you two would really get along. My treat," he added hastily, not forgetting her "steady income" jibe.

She tilted her head downward and peered up at him from beneath raised eyebrows. "That's sweet, Mitch, but I think I'll pass. Third Wheel isn't really my style."

"It's not like that."

"Yes, it *is* like that. Isn't she the one you hooked up with?"

"Yes, but that's ancient history now."

"Sure."

"It is," he protested. "She's actually been seeing another guy. This tool I used to go to high school with, JP." He couldn't keep the frustration out of his voice.

"Jealous much?"

Mitch's face remained expressionless as he continued to sort bottle caps. "Even if I were, what does it matter? She's seeing someone else."

Darcy added a few brushstrokes to the portrait. "Is she married to the guy? No. Unless she's married to the guy, she's fair game."

"Kate doesn't want to go out with me."

"How do you know that?"

"It's been pretty clear. She practically left skidmarks on my bedroom floor trying to get out the door the next day. Didn't even kiss me goodbye."

"Maybe she panicked."

"Eh, maybe. Anyway, we talked about it afterwards, and

we agreed to just be friends."

"Whose idea was that, yours or hers?"

"I don't know," he cleared his throat. "I guess I was doing most of the talking, maybe."

"So you never actually asked her out?"

"No," he admitted, rubbing the back of his neck with one hand.

"But you liked her!" Darcy threw her hands up, flicking paint across the room. "And you still like her. You're a bonehead."

Mitch sighed. "You may be right. But what's to be done about it now? Like I said, she's seeing someone else. They had their second date over the weekend. She told me so herself last night at Donovan's."

"Second date? A second date is nothing! And you sound like a broken record. *She's seeing someone else, she's seeing someone else*," Darcy mimicked. "Here's what's to be done: ASK HER OUT. She barely knows this other guy compared to you. Tell her how you feel. Maybe you're right and she doesn't like you, but maybe she does. You'll never know if you don't ask."

Mitch's phone buzzed, and he pulled it out of his back pocket, grateful for the interruption. "Speak of the devil."

Darcy smiled slyly. "Oh, really? What does she say?"

"She wants to know if I have plans for my birthday. It's coming up, the weekend before Halloween. October 28."

Darcy arched an eyebrow at him and crossed her arms over her chest, tilting her head to one side. "And you think she's not interested. Uh-huh."

Mitch let that one slide as he contemplated what to reply. Maybe Darcy was right; maybe now was the time to step up and do something about his feelings for Kate. And maybe his birthday would be the perfect day to do it.

21 ~ KEEPIN' IT KATE: "A DOG'S DINNER"

~October 12~

So there I am in The New Man's kitchen (I can't really call him Boyfriend yet, I think), minding my own water-boiling business, when in comes Big Dog, The New Man's not-so-small canine companion. Great. The first night I try to cook a nice dinner for us, and Big Dog decides to run interference. Have you ever tried to watch pots on the stove when there's a large, curious canine underfoot, begging for your attention? It's a bit tricky. Here's how it went down:

5:45 pm: The plan materializes: three-cheese tortellini with pasta sauce, pre-made salad in a bag, and hot, crusty garlic bread fresh outta the freezer. Can't be that complicated, right? (Famous last words.)

5:55 pm: Preheat the oven for the garlic bread. Finish washing the crusty dishes left in Boyfriend's sink. Did I need those dishes for this particular meal? No, but ugh, they were gross. No doubt I'm enabling Boyfriend and his untidy roommates by cleaning up their mess, but what can I say? I need a clean kitchen to get started.

5:56 pm: Water on to boil for the pasta. Open jar of pasta sauce (chunky tomato, onion, and garlic). Magically, Big Dog appears. Does Big Dog give me any warning that he's in the room? No. Big Dog scares the bejeezus out of me when I turn around and see him staring me down like one-third of Cerberus ready to pounce. Cue shrieking. Glass jar plummets to kitchen floor, shattering into fifty kajillion pieces and splattering sauce from one end of Hell's half-acre to the other.

5:58 pm: I wrap up a blue-streak of cursing and proceed to clean up the mess. Big Dog "helps" by licking sauce off my ankles with his sandpaper tongue. (Okay, I didn't mind that part so much—it tickled.) Garlic bread goes into the oven.

6:09 pm: Floor mopped. Cabinets wiped. Stained slacks and blouse soaking in the bathroom sink. I'm now wearing a pair of Boyfriend's faded sweatpants and a plain white undershirt from his plain-white-undershirt drawer. Seriously? How many plain white undershirts does one person need? At this point, the water on stove has not only begun to boil, but has steamed away while I was busy cleaning, leaving only two inches in the bottom of the pot. Not enough to cook tortellini. *Shit.* Add more water, put pot back on to boil. Big Dog, meanwhile, watches the scene somewhat quizzically. It's possible that Big Dog has never seen cooking (or cleaning, for that matter) in Boyfriend's house.

6:16 pm: Water boiling, tortellini on to cook. Big Dog gets pretty excited that there seems to be food in the works. He tries to jump up onto the stove to get a good look. I narrowly avoid plunging my hand into scorching water as I run pass interference between dog and pot.

6:19 pm: Realize I now have no sauce to go with the tortellini, and it's too late to take the tortellini out of the water, as it's almost done cooking. *Shit*, Part Deux. Tearing apart of the cabinets begins, searching for ingredients that could, in some stretch of the imagination, be transformed into pasta sauce. Big Dog gets excited at this flurry of activity. Much barking ensues. Oh joy.

6:21 pm: Tortellini comes off the stove and into a serving dish until further notice.

6:24 pm: One small can of sliced black olives, a small jar of pizza sauce, and a value-size jug of "hot 'n' spicy" giardiniera—carrots, cauliflower, red pepper, hot pepper rings. That's about all the search turns up. Slim pickings. I reluctantly conclude that while these ingredients might make a fairly kick-ass muffaletta, they'll never work for tortellini (or at least, I don't know how to make them work for tortellini), and I have neither salami nor ciabatta for muffaletta. #FirstWorldProblems, amiright? So now I'm thinking maybe I'll just sauté some onions and garlic in butter to dress the pasta. That might work, if I can find some olive oil.

6:26 pm: Chopped onion is in the sauté pan, sloshing in some of Italy's first cold-pressed finest. Powdered garlic will have to do, as that's all there is. About this time, Big Dog decides that barking and weaving between my legs is not enough. He "playfully" nips the sensitive flesh of my lower calf. Surprise! I'm hopping around on one leg now, waving my arms like a maniac and involuntarily yelling in pain. I manage to knock the pasta off the countertop and onto the floor, where it lands face-down with a gunshot *crack* of the dish. *Shit*, Part Three. First thought: *I hope that wasn't his mom's dish.* Second thought: *Maybe I could serve it anyway, if I can pick out all the broken pieces.* After all, I know the floor's clean.

30 seconds later: Smoke detector goes off. *Shit*, Part...Four? I don't know, I've lost count at this point. The garlic bread. Pull open oven door, black smoke rolls out. Yum, carbon.

6:27 pm: Using broom handle, I manage to silence blaring

alarm on the ceiling. Unfortunately, I bash it too hard. It now hangs down by a noose of white electrical cords. Mmm, someone's gonna notice that.

6:29 pm: I cave and order pizza from a magnet on the refrigerator. (It must be the usual joint if there's a fridge magnet, right?) We're having Italian for dinner one way or the other tonight, damnit. Big Dog guilt-trips me with the saddest eyes ever as I clean up the spilled pasta. He doesn't understand what wee sharp bits could do to his insides; all he knows is that something mighty tasty is going into the garbage, without him sampling a single bite of this unknown delight.

But what to do with all that sautéed onion? I start to laugh hysterically. And that, of course, is the moment that The New Man gets back from the gym. Sulky dog, pasta and broken glass everywhere, girlfriend in cruddy duds and sweaty from exertion, smoke detector dangling from the ceiling, and the reek of onions and garlic in the air.

But wait! There's good news. He's got take-out Chinese in one hand.

Some nights, two dinners is just what the doctor ordered.

22 ~ PINEAPPLE INSIDE-OUT DATE

~ October 27 ~

JP leaned into the trunk of his car and pulled out the overstuffed cardboard box. A jumble of sweaters and knickknacks threatened to spill out over the top. Kate followed him into the donation center, where he set the box on the counter. It was whisked away by an efficient volunteer, already eyeing up the contents.

"Let's go!" JP tugged on her arm excitedly, leading her to the front entrance of the thrift shop, just around the corner from the donation center. He pulled open the door eagerly and they stepped inside.

"What exactly are we looking for again?" she asked, slightly puzzled.

He chuckled. "You don't come to the thrift store to look for things. You come to the thrift store to find things."

JP spied an aisle chock full of sling-back chairs, camping stoves, tents, and sleeping bags. Camping season had wrapped up for the year, so it was the perfect time to snap up bargain cast-offs. Kate, meanwhile, found her eye drawn to the shelves of books on the other side of the store. Usually, she trolled garage sales and used book stores, but maybe she'd find something good here. She made a beeline for the display. With a speculative eye, she pulled out copies one at a time, searching for first editions. Well-known authors only, in mint condition; those were

116

her criteria. Anything else went back on the shelf.

Ten minutes later, she struck gold. "By cracky!" she squealed, turning more than one head in her direction. Her hand shot out to capture a kelly green book off the shelf: *The Book of Lost Tales*, by J.R.R. Tolkien. Not one of his best-known works, but it looked to be in great condition. Quickly, Kate flipped through the pages, looking for any major stains, tears, or water damage, but the book was pristine. Even the dust jacket barely showed any use; just the usual shelf wear around the edges. Kate couldn't wait to add it to her growing collection. *One more book closer to my dream library.*

She ran off to hunt down JP. "Look!" she shoved the book under his nose, her hand shaking with excitement. "A first edition Tolkien, and for a DOLLAR! I think I'm gonna like this thrift store thing!"

"Awesome! So, does this mean you're rich now?" he joshed, putting his arm around her shoulders and giving her an exaggerated squeeze.

"Ha! Probably not. A book like this might be worth twenty or thirty bucks, but not much more than that. Still, it's a nice find."

"I had no idea you were such a bibliophile."

"I had no idea you knew the word *bibliophile*."

"Learn something new every day, don't you?"

"I guess so. What about you? Did you find anything good?"

"Yep. Take a gander at this," he said, looking quite pleased. He held up an iron square welded to the top of two metal sticks.

"Oh, it's a...um..." Kate fumbled to identify the unknown piece of equipment.

"Pi'iron!"

"A piron?"

"A pie iron," he enunciated, opening his mouth widely for each word.

"Of course, a pie iron." Her blank look made it obvious that she hadn't a clue what a pie iron was.

He blinked at her incredulously. "You don't know what a pie iron is?"

"I'm guessing you don't use it to iron pies."

He chortled. "Nope! You cook with it. Over a fire. Sometimes pies, but lots of other stuff, too. Mostly I use it to make sandwiches. It's really simple. Just put in two pieces of bread and whatever filling you want, put it in the fire for a few minutes, and you've got yourself some dinner."

"Huh." Camping wasn't really Kate's thing. She hadn't grown up in one of those outdoorsy families, the kind where the dad taught the boys how to tie fishing lures and the mom whipped up gourmet meals in a cast iron skillet. Oh no. In her family, the closest they got to The Great Outdoors was standing in line to see the bears at the zoo once a year.

"We'll have to try it out sometime! I make a mean Pineapple Inside-Out Cake."

Kate perked up. "Sweets? Now you've got my attention! That sounds yummy."

"It's ridiculous!" he promised. "One cake donut, sliced in half, a ring of pineapple in the middle, and some butter and brown sugar. Put that sucker in the pie iron, and wham, dessert. It's even better with a scoop of vanilla ice cream on top, though that's usually hard to come by when you're camping."

"It just so happens that I have some vanilla ice cream at home, *and* a fire pit on the back deck."

Thirty minutes later, after paying for their treasures and a quick stop for groceries, Kate found herself slicing donuts in the kitchen while JP stoked the fire out back. She hummed to herself and smiled; she was never so happy as when dessert was on the horizon. Even better than that, dessert with this sexy, funny man who seemed to be settling in as her boyfriend. Life was pretty good. Finally, it looked like things were going her way.

* * * * *

The fire burned low, its quiet hiss giving way to an errant pop every now and then. Kate snuggled further back into JP's embrace, resting against his chest, her head tucked just below his chin. Despite the undeniable chill in the air, she felt toasty warm, inside and out. The pie iron had lived up to the hype; Kate was thoroughly blissed-out on a carbohydrate high of caramelized cake donuts, pineapple, and ice cream. They quietly sipped their Irish coffees.

"Kate?" His voice was low, drifting down to her ears like a lullaby.

"Mmm?"

"I'm really glad I met you." The heart Kate had been keeping on cool reserve against JP's charm began to melt just a trickle.

"Me, too, JP." She tilted her head back for a tender kiss.

"I wonder what I would be doing right now if I hadn't met you," she mused. "Whatever it is, I'm sure it wouldn't be half as wonderful as this."

He kissed her again, with increasing intensity. Things were getting too close for comfort. Kate couldn't understand her hesitation. *Isn't this what I wanted?* Gingerly, she disentangled herself from JP's arms and pushed up from the lounge chair, gathering dishes to take into the house.

"Leave those." His voice was a soft request. She felt the light touch of his hand wrap around her wrist, and then she was in his arms, melting into a warm, inviting kiss. JP waltz-kissed her across the wooden boards, holding her close and turning her round and round until she laughed in delight.

Kate could feel the heat spreading across her cheeks— and everywhere else. She gently pushed him away and opened the sliding glass door, taking much longer than needed to remove her jacket and hang it on the coat tree near the front. She moved toward the kitchen, putting some space between them. "Something to drink?"

"Sure, what have you got?" JP closed the distance between them in three easy strides. His arm gently encircled her waist to detain her, and he eased forward until they stood in a close embrace. His mouth, only inches away, lowered down to nuzzle hers again. He took his time, one small kiss after another. Kate's head spun, nearly chasing all thoughts away completely...

...all thoughts except for slowing things down just a bit. "I think I've got just the thing. Hold that thought." He released her, and she disappeared into the kitchen.

Digging through the fridge, she found was she was looking for: a bottle of chocolate porter she'd been saving for just such an occasion. Smooth and creamy, with a hint of vanilla; the perfect dessert beer—and the perfect way to end a perfect date. Kate poured out the richly scented, dark liquid into two glasses and floated back to the living room. JP was lounging on the couch in front of the fireplace, lights already dimmed. *Man, he's smooth.* She drank in his lean frame, stretched out comfortably in a reclining pose, and she imagining what it would be like to strip off those layers of jacket, shirt, slacks... Her mouth watered. *Now that's what I call "Mmm, mmm, good!"*

The flicker of flames from the hearth glinted off the glass as Kate handed it to her date. A slow smile crept across his face as he reached up to accept the drink with one hand and capture her hand with the other. He tugged slightly, an invitation to settle in close to him. Easing herself into a comfortable position, she snuggled up against JP's lean-muscled side. One arm slipped around her shoulders and he hugged her lightly to his body. Kate rested her head on his shoulder for a moment, smiling softly.

"Cheers," she toasted, raising her glass to his with a clink. They tasted the rich brew in silence, holding each other's gaze as the spark between them slowly flared to life.

"Delicious," he murmured, taking a sip. "I can think of something else I'm pretty sure is delicious, too," he hinted, his eyes tracing a path down to the top button of her shirt. "May I?"

Kate let out a small, hot breath. *What am I hesitating for, anyway? Mitch and I are obviously a "never were" and a "never gonna be." And it's like they say,* she convinced herself, *the best way to get over someone is to get under someone else.* She met the carnal question in JP's eyes and nodded, permission granted.

JP's mouth curled into a smile of satisfaction. He reached up to release one button, then slowly peeled back the fabric to uncover the swell of her breasts. Kate swallowed as he lowered his head and brushed delicate kisses across the exposed flesh. "Mmmm," was all she could manage, the low sound of pleasure bringing JP's eyes back to her face again.

"You're so beautiful..." He dusted kisses along her jawline, working his way up to the sensitive flesh behind her ear. His warm breath stirred locks of her hair, tickling her neck and further adding to her heightened state.

"Come here," he invited, urging her even closer. Kate curled her body across him, his breath stirring the crown of her head. "I've thought you were beautiful from the moment I laid eyes on you."

Kate snapped out of her reverie and snorted in sharp laughter. "Ha! You mean the moment when you hit me in the face with a sweaty basketball?" A deep laugh rumbled from inside his chest.

"Heh heh! Yeah, sorry about that. I didn't mean to hit you in the face. I only wanted to get your attention."

"What?!" She sat upright and scooched off his lap. "You mean that wasn't an accident?" She laughed. "At last, the truth comes out: JP Sampson picks up women by assaulting them with sporting goods." She crossed her arms and pursed her lips in mock outrage.

"Awww, come on, Kate," he soothed, quite contrite in appearance—except for that wanton gleam in his eye. "I said I was sorry. Should I beg for your forgiveness?" He dropped down to his knees before her on the couch, hands caressing her thighs indolently. "What can I do to make it up to you?" he beseeched her in a comical mix of feigned regret and lewdness.

She grinned. "Well," she hedged innocently, rolling her eyes heavenward as if in deep contemplation, "I suppose I could think of a thing or two..."

JP smiled a wicked smile. "I know just where to start," he declared, slowly levering her knees apart with his broad, strong hands. *Oh my...!*

23 ~ Bagels, Bull Dancers, and Booze

~ October 28 ~

Today is the day! Mitch hummed "Happy Birthday" to himself as he practically skipped up the street. It had taken him a while to figure things out, but now he knew exactly what he wanted: Kate. He didn't want to be "just friends" anymore. *What have I been waiting for? Kate and I are perfect for each other.*

JP swooping in and stealing Kate away had been just the reality check he'd needed. Seeing Kate with the wrong man yet again had made Mitch realize just how right Darcy was; he needed to grab life by the balls and just go for it. *When will I ever find another woman like Kate? Never.* Nobody made him laugh the way that she did. Nobody knew him as well as she did. And nobody could hold a candle to her, either—at least, as far as he was concerned.

Mitch had barely seen Kate in over two weeks now, aside from grabbing a quick lunch or two in the cafeteria between design-team meetings. He'd been swamped at work lately, pulling together mock-ups for the upcoming Christmas campaign. Kate seemed to have fallen off the radar, too. Even their usual Monday night dinners had temporarily fallen to the wayside. All the more reason that

Mitch had been looking forward to today—a chance to reconnect and spend some quality time together.

His nerves sizzled as he touched a hand to the pocket on the front of his broadcloth shirt. *Phew, it's still there.* It wasn't an engagement ring, but it was still a ring. His class ring, from college. Maybe it was silly and old-fashioned, and they were long past college, but he wanted Kate to wear it. He'd never asked a girl to wear it before, even Camille. But he wanted to know that Kate was his and only his. *I don't suppose people use the phrase "go steady" anymore, but if it was good enough for Mom and Dad, it's good enough for me. Look at how long their love lasted.* His eyes misted over for just a moment, but in happiness. He was glad his parents had enjoyed so many years of deep love and close companionship, even though it had ended all too soon.

An exhilarated smile spread across his face as he hustled up the street toward the café. He couldn't wait to be with Kate, and to finally tell her how much she meant to him. He knew now that he had loved her for years. His feelings had been impossible to ignore since that day she showed up on his doorstep, soup and wontons in hand.

He had the day perfectly planned for them. First, a trip to the art museum to take in an exhibit of the Romantics. What could be better than a morning of Delacroix, Waterhouse, and Friedrich to stir the passions and set the stage for a declaration of love? After the museum, lunch—at Harry's Dim-Sum a-Go-Go, of course. He hadn't planned anything for after lunch. *If things go well...* His heart leaped in his chest and a burst of energy surged through him just daydreaming about it. Today might be the day he would make Kate his own—this time, for good.

Yes, today is going to be a great day!

* * * * *

Kate inhaled a mouthful of latte with a satisfied slurp, unable to wipe the smug grin off her face. *I wonder if everyone here can tell we just had sex last night?* She eyeballed the crowd at the bustling breakfast joint just around the corner from her condo. *And by "we," I mean me and this drop-dead gorgeous hunk of a man. Yeah, that's right, ladies. Don't be hatin'.* She couldn't help but notice the envious glances cast her way by some of the nearby females.

JP looked calm and relaxed as always, perfectly in control of himself and the situation. He popped a bite of croissant into his mouth with an appreciative "mmm," then glanced across the table and caught Kate's eye. He flashed that breathtaking smile of his, reaching over to squeeze her hand with warmth. "I had an amazing time last night," he flirted in a hushed voice, raising his eyebrows subtlely.

"Me too," she said, blushing a bit as her smile got even bigger. She buried her nose in her mug, hoping the steam rising from it would camouflage her face.

"I want to spend more time with you, Kate."

"I'd like that." Once again, JP was making this easy on her. *How nice it is to have a man just say what he wants, plain and simple.* She wondered if things would always be this uncomplicated with JP, but she wasn't about to second-guess it at this point. She'd done far too much over-thinking when it came to the men in her life. This time, she was just going to sail with the breeze and see where it carried her.

A harsh, metallic buzzing interrupted her train of thought. A text was coming in, vibrating her phone across the table. Annoyed, she clicked the phone off and stuck it in her purse. *Nobody needs to get ahold of me at this time of day on a Saturday morning. Whoever it is can wait.* She gave JP her full attention as they chatted about each other's plans for the week and continued their leisurely meal.

*   *   *   *   *

Hmm, that's weird. She hasn't texted me back. She's probably still sleeping. Ruh roh, Raggy! Waking up Kate was never a fun proposition. *Guess I'd better get us some coffee.*

Mitch pushed open the door to the café, knowing that Kate without coffee in the morning was a Kate nobody should have to face. Although the place was fairly busy, there was nobody waiting in line to order. *My lucky day, indeed!* he grinned, as he stepped up to order two large French roasts. "To go, please. And throw in a couple of sesame bagels, toasted, with veggie cream cheese on the side. Thanks." Kate's favorite. *That oughta put a smile on her face.* And that was when Mitch felt a hearty wallop on his back between his shoulder blades.

*   *   *   *   *

Kate's fork was just breaking through the flaky crust of her blueberry tart when she felt the hairs on the back of her neck stand up. Her head turned toward the door instinctively.

Mitch?! Why is he here? Kate's gut constricted with guilt, even though she'd done nothing wrong. During the months that had passed since their night together, Mitch had never once said or even hinted that he wanted to be with her. *Moving on with someone else is for the best. I can't pine for Mitch indefinitely, even if he is a great guy and a great friend.* Mitch stood at the counter, happily oblivious. *Maybe he won't see us,* she fervently hoped.

JP noticed the odd look on Kate's face and followed her gaze across the café. The next second, he was out of his chair and giving Mitch a huge "hey pal" slap on the back. *Damn.* Kate shrank in her seat.

"Mitch, hey!" JP boomed. His loud voice carried throughout the suddenly stuffy room, causing heads to turn their way.

Mitch sized up the long-limbed man in front of him, suffering the momentary disorientation of meeting an acquaintance outside the usual context. "JP?" he blurted out. "What are you doing here?"

"We were just having breakfast," he said in a jolly voice. Kate cringed, wishing she could melt into the floor as JP waved a hand in her direction. He had no clue of her history with Mitch, beyond the fact that they were old friends. *Could this get any more awkward?*

"Kate?" She saw an astonished Mitch mouth her name, the din of the restaurant drowning him out. Slowly, he made his way over to the table where she cowered, trying unsuccessfully to shrink away into oblivion.

"Hi, Mitch," she smiled wanly.

"Kate." His tone was flat, devoid of warmth or any feeling at all.

*   *   *   *   *

"Mitch, hey!" boomed a cheery male voice that was undoubtedly connected to the overzealous back thump. He turned to face his high-spirited assailant. Tall, very tall...*I know this guy*...grey eyes, ridiculous butt chin...*oh hell*. Of all the people he really didn't want to run into in real life, here was number one.

"We were just having breakfast," JP said, pointing across the brunching crowd to where the woman herself sat, looking as if she'd just swallowed a fly. Her name came to his lips, but the sound stuck in his throat. His legs moved of their own volition, dragging him over to the table to face the woman he loved—the woman who had no idea of her place in his heart.

Cool words floated to his ear. "Hi, Mitch." *I swear, her face is green. What is she doing here with that tool, anyway?* Deep down, he already knew the answer. A storm whirled in his head. The thought of someone else— anyone else—making love to Kate made bile rise to his throat. The fact that it was JP made it even worse.

"Kate." His voice cracked a bit as JP slid into the seat opposite her. Then she asked the question which revealed just how little Mitch really meant to her.

"What are you doing here?"

He could see the genuine confusion on her face. *She forgot. She totally forgot. I guess I'm the real tool here. Here I am, planning this glorious day for us in which I declare my eternal love and devotion, and she doesn't even remember we had plans. What a giant moron I am! How could I have been so incredibly dense?*

*   *   *   *   *

"What are you doing here?" Kate asked, at a loss.

"I guess you forgot," Mitch said. "Didn't you get my text? I thought you were just still asleep, so I stopped in to get us some breakfast."

Kate wanted to smack herself on the forehead. "It's *today*?"

"Yeah," he said quietly. "It's today."

"Omigod, I'm so sorry, I completely forgot!" Kate was truly flustered now.

Mitch could almost hide his bitter expression, but not quite. "Don't worry about it. You're obviously busy here." His voice was a bucket of ice water dumped over Kate's head. She sat in stunned silence as he turned on his heel to leave.

"Oh, wait," he turned back. "I got this one for you." He shoved a tumbler of coffee into her hand. "But I'm keeping the bagels. It's my birthday, after all." The knife twisted in her heart as he stalked out the door.

"Eek," JP looked both bemused and concerned. "What in the world was that?" he asked, perplexed. In her head, Kate was still reciting *Oh shit, oh shit, oh shit, oh shit...* until it came bursting out of her mouth.

"Oh shit! I am a terrible, terrible person and a bad, bad friend. It's Mitch's birthday! I can't believe I forgot. We were supposed to go to the museum together. Ugh, now I feel terrible!" In a shot, she was out of her seat. "I'm sorry, JP," she called over her shoulder. "I've got to go! I'll call you later! And thanks for breakfast..." her voice drifted back to him as she raced out the door.

*   *   *   *   *

Kate flounced down the street after the retreating figure of Mitch, rapidly disappearing from view. "Mitch, will you wait a minute?" she cried, panting from the run. She caught up to him just as he reached his car.

Mitch pivoted on one heel toward her and leaned back against his car, his face a study in stoic reserve. He lifted one eyebrow a fraction of an inch, but said nothing.

Kate struggled for words, her mouth gaping open uselessly. "I, uh...I..."

"What, nothing clever to say?" Mitch set his mouth in a firm line of exasperation, a low-grade expression of hurt and anger brewing beneath the surface.

Kate's heart plummeted as she realized the extent of the damage she'd done. She felt about two inches tall. "Mitch, I am *so* sorry that I forgot we had plans today. I feel awful." She looked up at him hopefully. His face was still stony.

"I can see you're mad at me, and you have every right to be. I'm so sorry, really. Let me make it up to you!" she coaxed. "We can go to the museum, lunch, and anywhere else you want to go, too."

Mitch shoved his hands in his coat pockets and looked speculatively at Kate as she stood by, anxiously awaiting his reply. He weighed his options, still trying to get a handle on his anger. He knew it wasn't his birthday he was mad about, though. *How could she have slept with someone else? I haven't been able to even look at another woman since we were together!*

His conscience broke in. *That was months ago, pal. What was she supposed to do? Just sit around and wait for you—after you told her you just wanted to be friends?* Unconsciously, his hand drifted to his shirt pocket, where the ring now weighed him down like a lump of lead. *I really blew it this time. I waited too long, and now she's found someone else. It's too late for this ring. Too late for us.* Melancholy washed over him, draining the life from his eyes.

Kate was still awaiting his response anxiously, her hands balled into tight knots of tension. At last, he let out a long breath and spoke.

"It's okay," he yielded, his voice low. Relief flooded her face and a grateful smile replaced her worried frown. "It still sucks that you forgot my birthday, but I guess it happens. People forget things. Birthdays aren't really that big of a deal anyway. NOT that I won't let you make it up to me."

Kate flung her arms around his neck. "Thanks, Mitch. You're the best friend ever!" A splintering of tears prickled the corners of his eyes as he returned her embrace. Blinking them away rapidly, he buried his head into her hair and breathed deeply. She smelled like rose petals; her scent comforted him. Just being close to her made his problems seem a million miles away. *This is how it should always be*, he thought happily for a moment, before reality set in again. *But this isn't how it really is. It's just a fantasy that will never come true.* Icy regret filled the area where his heart used to beat. Reluctantly, he dropped his arms back to his sides. *So much for "Today is the day."*

* * * * *

Mitch stepped into Exhibit Hall number one-hundred-and-seventy-trillion, feeling rather weary. As much as he loved art, he'd had his fill for one day. The day wasn't going the way he'd planned at all—not after this morning's revelation that Kate was doing the pants-dance with someone else. *I should be kissing my girlfriend right now*, he thought sourly. *Instead I'm yesterday's news.*

"Check this one out," Kate called him over. She was studying a reproduction of an ancient fresco.

"That's one crazy rodeo going on there." He examined the figure of an obviously insane man doing a flip over the back of a charging bull.

"It's a bull dancer, from the island of Crete. Bulls were sacred to the people there. This must be from Knossos." She scrutinized the information card tacked to the wall beside the display and confirmed her hunch. "Bull-dancing was a kind of entertainment, believe it or not."

"Gee, sounds like fun. Not. These Greek folks of yours sound like they might've had a couple of screws loose." He whirled one finger at his temple to show how crazy it sounded to him.

Kate was too absorbed in the rich turquoise, reds, and golds of the fresco to pay his mockery any mind. "How exciting it must have been, watching these young athletes hurl themselves toward the bull, feet flying, then grabbing onto the horns and catapulting over! Now *that* would be one heck of an Olympic sport."

"Ha! I don't think you'd get too many takers for that nowadays."

"Oh, I don't know. Look at all the crazy folks who run with the bulls in Pamplona every year."

He laughed out loud, startling some of the other patrons nearby. A sheepish look spread across his face and he whispered a hushed "Sorry" to the other occupants as he took Kate's arm and guided her into the next room.

Immediately, Kate was drawn to a dramatic oil painting on the far side of the gallery. "Mitch, look! It's Orpheus and Eurydice." She leaned close to examine the tortured lover and his lady. Mitch had no clue what Kate was talking about.

"And they would be...?" he asked, ready to be enlightened.

Kate's face turned dreamy, her eyes softening, giving her a more vulnerable air. "They were in love," she said softly, venturing a quick glance in Mitch's direction to find that she had his undivided attention. Unexpectedly, she felt butterflies in her stomach. Quickly, she turned back to the painting and continued her story. "Orpheus was a great musician, and Eurydice was his wife. It was love at first sight. He was enamored of her beauty, and she was spellbound by his songs. But then poor Eurydice died."

"That must be what's in the picture, then." Mitch examined the wretched man, his arms reaching out to catch the fainting beauty as she crumpled.

"No, not exactly," said Kate. "Eurydice died of a snake bite, actually. When Orpheus found her dead in the forest, he journeyed all the way to the Underworld to try to win her life back. He played such sad songs that even the gods wept. Hades finally relented and allowed him to take his wife back to earth. There was one condition, though." She swallowed and glanced over at him, as if reluctant to continue to the unhappy end.

"Which was?" Mitch looked at her thoughtfully,

noticing how visibly affected she was by the myth. Her lower lip trembled just a touch before she resumed the story.

"He wasn't allowed to look back at her until they were both safely out of the Underworld and into the light of day. Orpheus led the way, and she followed. They were almost there when, I guess he couldn't help himself..."

"...he turned around," Mitch finished quietly.

"...and she disappeared from his arms, forever," Kate concluded somberly. "Gods, what a story! The Greeks really were the masters of tragedy. Is there anything sadder than finding the one you love, only to lose them through your own stupid mistake?"

"No," he answered, the word a block of lead on his tongue. "I can't think of anything in the world worse than that." Now his gloomy demeanor matched her own. But while Kate merely felt sympathy for poor Orpheus, Mitch was feeling the true pain of his story.

"Kate..." he began, surprising himself as the unplanned words sprang to his lips: *You're my Eurydice.* But he couldn't say them. Now that he finally had the courage to tell her how he felt, she was no longer his to tell.

She cast her emotion-stirred eyes on him, the effects of the tragic love story still churning in their hazel depths. "Yes?"

Mitch faltered. "I...was just wondering who the artist was. I might like to buy a postcard of this one at the gift shop."

She blinked, coming back to reality a bit. "Oh, right. Let me see. The card says George Frederick Watts, on loan from some gallery in Massachusetts."

"Great. I'll keep an eye out for it."

Kate moved on to the next gallery. Mitch trailed behind her, pausing to give the painting a brief parting glance. He offered a heartbroken goodbye, just as the man portrayed had bid adieu to his lost love. *You and me, Orpheus. You and me.*

* * * * *

"...So, JP, huh?" Mitch asked awkwardly as he and Kate exited the building.

"Yeah," Kate said with some hesitation. "I know, it's weird, isn't it?"

"Not a match I would have expected, that's for sure. I mean, you guys seemed to hit it off well enough at the gym, but I never thought you'd still be hanging out with him."

"Mmm," Kate answered without really answering.

"You guys don't really seem to have much in common. But I suppose there could be more to JP than I know."

Kate had to smile a little at that one. "No, probably not. JP's pretty much an open book. There's not much about him that you can't figure out within the first ten minutes of meeting him. That's one of the reasons I like him: he's easy to read. I've never had to wonder where I stand with him or how he feels." *Unlike some people.*

Mitch frowned subtly. *Ouch. Was that directed at me?*

"You're right, though—we don't really have that much in common. But we always have a good time together. We never run out of things to talk about, and he's seems like a decent guy."

Mitch grunted.

"What? You don't think so?"

He shrugged, looking up at the clouds and avoiding her piercing gaze. "I don't know, Kate. He was kind of a womanizer in high school. Every week, a new girl..."

"That was a long time ago. Don't you think it's possible that he might have changed?"

"It's possible, I suppose. But I'd still be careful, if I were you."

"Don't you worry, I can handle JP. Besides, we're just dating. It's not like it's super serious or anything yet."

Sleeping with someone isn't super serious?! Mitch's mind reeled. Kate was fooling herself if she really believed that. He knew for a fact that she hadn't been with that many guys, and getting involved with JP was like playing with fire.

"Hey, it's none of my business, really," he tried to disown the conversation. "If it makes you happy, I guess that's all that matters."

Suddenly, he couldn't imagine sitting through lunch with Kate. A lunch in which he did not, in fact, declare his undying love for her, but rather had to pretend to be happy for her and the new man in her life.

"Hey, do you mind if we take a rain check on lunch? My mom called last night and sounded kind of lonely. I think I might drive out there and surprise her."

"That's so sweet. I'm sure she'll love that. Hey, are you coming to the Halloween party tonight? Everyone will be there. George, Cecie, Evette—the whole gang."

"I'm gonna pass. I think Mom could use the company, actually."

"Well, all right. Have fun with your mom, then. And happy birthday, Mitch." She gave him a quick hug as he turned to go.

"Thanks. I'll see you Monday at work." He retreated to his car as quickly as possible, not wanting to prolong the goodbyes. *Fun with my mom is not exactly what I had in mind for this afternoon, but at least I know I can make one woman's day.*

* * * * *

It was only 9:30 and there was already a drunken mummy passed out on the front lawn of The Shithole. This run-down abode on the edge of campus had been Party Central ever since Kate could remember. As each resident (eventually) graduated, some new undergrad rose up to claim his vacant room in the house and keep the party rolling. Cecie's husband, George, had lived in the house once upon a time, and now he'd passed on the torch to his younger brother, Damon.

Kate shook her head at the mummy and laughed. "Yep, that's about par for the course for Trick-or-Drink." Trick-or-Drink was the unsanctioned (and highly frowned-upon) party that erupted each year at Ohiowa State, a school known more for its boozy reputation than its academic one. Nothing much had changed since Kate's college days. The same buzz of overexcited hormones crackled in the air as co-eds wandered the streets in costumes strange and wondrous. Scantily clad nurses and warrior princesses, pimps-n-hoes, vampires, superheroes, zombies, pirates, and of course, zombie pirates roamed the sidewalks in a spectacle of people-watching.

"Tell me again why we're going to a campus party?" JP couldn't hide his disgust at the drooling mummy passed out in the grass, the empty beer bottles littering the porch, and the table-banging sound of a rousing game of Thumper coming from inside the dilapidated house.

"Oh, come on. It'll be fun."

"I have the sneaking suspicion that your idea of fun and my idea of fun may not intersect on this one."

Kate gave him a sassy little pout and leaned forward just a tad, offering up an ample view of the bountiful cleavage tucked away inside her snug red-and-gold bodice. His eyes traveled downward to the skin-tight lycra pants in royal blue and the knee-high boots that elevated her frame five inches off the ground.

JP licked his lips in appreciation. "You do make a smashing Wonder Woman, though, and it's hard to argue with Wonder Woman." He reached out and hauled her snugly against his chest. "I know something else that's hard, too." He gave her a wolfish grin. "Damn, woman! You look so hot...are you sure you wouldn't rather have a private party of our own?" He slid his hands down the backside of her tight pants and began to assail her with kisses. Things got hot—fast. Kate wrapped one leg around him and he pressed against her, deepening the kiss. In a heartbeat, her back was up against the scratchy brick of the house. JP's hands threaded through her hair, his thumbs stroking the sensitive flesh on the back of her neck. There was no doubt whatsoever what was on JP's mind; his Men-in-Tights costume didn't do much to hide his excitement.

Bang! The screen door slammed sharply as a gaggle of intoxicated youths staggered out onto the porch for a mid-Thumper smoke break. Kate and JP broke apart with a start, titters of amusement greeting them. "Dude, get a room!" joked a nerdy guy in a brown sport coat and bowtie. He was obviously going for Dr. Who, but in reality looked more like Bill Nye the Science Guy.

Kate ducked out from behind JP and laced her fingers through his, giving a gentle tug toward the front door. She could still feel the blood pumping through her veins, and knew her cheeks must be scarlet, from both the kissing and the mortification of being caught in the act. "Come on, let's go," she said. *Before I change my mind and break about thirty public indecency laws out here.*

The inside of the house was just as Kate remembered it but even grungier, if that were possible. The scuffed wooden floors still hadn't been refinished, and the creaky wooden staircase with its rickety banister (perfect for sliding down, except for that bothersome finial at the end) was as creaky as ever. The dingy walls were pockmarked with nail holes and badly in need of a fresh coat of paint, and permeating everything was the faint scent of Swisher Sweets and wet dog.

JP cleared a path for them through the costume-clad partygoers in search of Kate's friends, finally locating them in the overcrowded kitchen. Cecie and George had, as usual, dressed themselves to match each other. George made a fine Roman gladiator, with his broad chest and hairy legs, while Cecie played it coy as a Vestal Virgin, draped in white robes and wearing a crown of leaves in her hair. Evette was not to be seen; Kate wondered if she had come at all.

Cecie's eyes widened as Kate introduced JP to the couple. "Goodness, you weren't exaggerating when you said that he was a hunk!" she gushed, gazing up slightly starry-eyed at JP, who blushed good-naturedly but flashed an appreciative glance Kate's way. Their eyes met warmly in a moment of mutual admiration.

"Don't let the Vestal Virgin costume fool you," Kate advised JP. "Cecie's the horniest woman I know."

"Kate!" Cecie protested, face registering shock and delight at the same time.

JP followed up instantly. "Virgin? Oh, I never would have guessed she was a virgin. I thought surely she must be Aphrodite, the Goddess of Love," he said smoothly, bowing and dusting a kiss on her outstretched hand. Cecie colored prettily at the over-the-top flattery, and Kate knew she was already won over.

"Lucky for you Cecie's a married woman," George muscled in, taking JP's hand away from his wife's and crushing it in his brawny grip, "or I'm afraid there'd be no way to keep her off you now." He winked with a broad grin.

"Phew, bullet dodged." JP clutched a hand to his chest and feigned a heart attack. "Thank goodness. One sexy, gorgeous woman is about all I can handle at a time." He planted a big kiss on Kate's lips, leaving her flustered. The crowd around them erupted in whoops and catcalls at her reddened face as the kiss broke apart.

"You guys again?" teased the Dr. Who wannabe, poking his nose in between Kate and JP and turning his head from one to the other with a comical *tsk tsk* noise. "Seriously, rooms are upstairs on the right. Try not to break anything." He winked and continued on his way.

"Gosh," Kate fanned herself, still blushing furiously. "Is it just me, or is it getting warm in here? All right, Mr. Chivalry, how about using all that charm to get me a drink?" He snapped to attention and bowed before her with a grand flourish.

"But of course, my dear. I shall return *tout de suite.*" Turning his head aside to Cecie, he quipped, "That's French for whenever the heck I can wade through that huge line at the keg. Anyone else for a cup of whatever first-class swill this joint is serving? No?" He grinned and was off.

Cecie spun around the instant he was gone. "Holy guacamole, Kate! Call out the fire brigade—that man is smokin' hot!"

"Don't worry, Kate's been putting out the fires back at the house," Evette crowed gleefully, appearing from the crowd just in time to poke her roommate in the ribs.

"Oh my God, you guys, stop!" Kate laughed. "You're embarrassing me."

"Nothing to be embarrassed about there," Evette countered, "except maybe for making your roommate wear earplugs last night." George let out a bellow of laughter, joined heartily by everyone in the group.

"No really, enough already," Kate gasped for air and put up a hand in submission. Then she smiled mischievously. "But yeah, it was a pretty good night, I can't lie. Not that you have any room to complain anyway, Vetta, with that dog of yours waking me at 6:00 a.m. every day wanting to go out and pee."

"Hey, it's not my fault I'm a sound sleeper. Drama's smart. He knows who to bug to get what he wants."

"Sounds like someone I know," Kate shot back. "I'm still not sure how we ended up with a dog in the household."

"I guess I'll leave you to think on that one!" Evette whirled away, whipping her bow and arrow behind her, a bad-ass Katniss Everdeen disappearing into the arena of costume co-eds.

"Better hope nobody tries out their Hunger Games moves with her tonight," Kate joked. "They're likely to get the business end of one of those arrows."

* * * * *

An hour later, Kate found herself deep in conversation with Damon, George's younger brother. Having settled into one corner of the ancient leather sofa in the living room, they were out of the line of fire as the party swirled around them full throttle. Kate sipped on her beer lightly, not only because she was D.D. for the night, but also because, well, it was really cheap beer.

"Archaeology? That's what I majored in!" Kate shouted over the din.

"Awesome! So what are you doing now?" he asked eagerly.

"Um, I uh..." Kate hemmed and hawed, but then realized there was no pretty way to put it. "I didn't find a job in the field when I graduated. I ended up in sales at The Pup is Up."

"Whoa. Stuck in Corporate America. That must be a drag."

Kate was sure he didn't mean to be rude, but man, were these youngsters blunt. "Yeah, kinda," she admitted. "But beggars can't be choosers. I needed a job when I graduated, and that's what I got. It's not all bad, but I never thought I'd still be there five years later. What about you? You're graduating next year, right? What's your game plan?"

"I'm doing what I can to beef up my resume. I've been doing internships every summer here in the States, mostly out west on dino digs. This year, though, I've got the Big Dig lined up. Field work in Athens, Greece," he beamed. "I get worked up just thinking about it! Can't wait—it'll be my first time overseas."

"That's amazing! Who's leading the dig?"

"Professor Jenkins."

"Seriously? He was my thesis advisor. I thought he retired."

"He did, but he still leads these summer gigs. Gives him something to do so he doesn't go crazy with boredom, I guess."

Kate stared down into her flimsy plastic cup, swirling the pale, flat liquid around and around. "Really, I'm jealous. I was supposed to go on a dig like that when I was a senior, but it didn't pan out. No pun intended." She flashed a crooked smile.

"You should come along! The trip isn't full yet, and it's not limited to undergrads. You could do it as Continuing Ed, I bet. We'll be based out of Athens, but working about 30 minutes out of town, in the countryside. It's a really cheap trip, too. Room and board are free for volunteers, and they're even giving us a little bit of spending money each week. All you've got to do is pony up for the plane ticket. And of course whatever you want to spend on tacky souvenirs," he snickered.

Kate was dazzled. For a few fleeting moments, she considered the possibility. Greece—Athens! Her dream dig, and all she had to do was say *yes*. Visions of all things Greek began to fill her mind: the Forum and the Acropolis, the golden mask of Agamemnon, calamari fresh from the sea and ouzo strong enough to knock your socks off (*blech!*), the rocky landscape and cliffside monasteries...it was all so gorgeous and romantic. *How could anyone resist?* Kate's face was alight with the possibilities, but then the glamour faded she shook her head, clearing away the impractical fog. "I can't do it," she sighed. "I've got a job, remember?"

"It's only four weeks. Couldn't they give you a little extra vacation time?"

She snorted. "Yeah, right. Even the company president only takes three weeks a year."

"Ugh, that's terrible." Damon looked defeated. "Well, I wish you could go. We'd have a blast."

"I'm sure we would." She smiled genuinely. "So tell me what you'll be doing on the dig." Kate did her best to listen with enthusiasm, but somehow, her heart just wasn't in it.

24 ~ Downward-Facing Dork

~ November 1 ~

How hard could it be? Kate asked herself nervously as she padded into the spartan studio in her bare feet. Nubile ladies (and a few gents) dotted the room, evenly spaced out and already seated on their brightly colored yoga mats. The light chatter of people comfortably acquainted with one another breezed around her ears. Kate had the distinct feeling of being the odd man out.

She tried to remain invisible as she crept to one corner and unrolled the thin, foam mat JP had loaned her. She wrinkled her nose as she spread it out on the polished wood floor. *It smells funny. Well, no matter. No doubt the room will soon be so full of B.O. that I won't be able to smell the mat anyway. How did he talk me into this, anyway? Ugh.*

Yoga was just about the last thing Kate had ever wanted to do. What was the point of contorting oneself into all those outlandish positions—except, of course, to be able to brag about being able to contort oneself into such outlandish positions? Oh sure, people joked about dating gymnasts and yoginis, but Kate had never had any complaints in the bedroom department, so she figured if it ain't broke, don't fix it. The only reason she was here was to be supportive of JP. He'd asked her to come, so what could she do but say yes?

The door opened and in came the man himself. A dreamy smile spread across Kate's face as she admired his lean, muscled physique, nicely set off by form-fitting grey yoga pants and an athletic tank in steel blue. Kate couldn't help but notice how virtually every girl in the room suddenly sat up just a little bit taller, presenting her best straight-backed form (breasts thrust forward, naturally) to this Adonis of an instructor. She gloated to herself just a tiny bit. *Yeah girls, you can look, but you can't touch. He's mine.* She started to perk up a bit. *Maybe this will be fun after all.*

Thirty minutes later, she realized how very deluded that thought had been. *Beginner's yoga? This is beginner's yoga?! Then why the heck does everyone look like they've been doing this for years already?* Kate squirmed with embarrassment at her own clumsy attempts to match the postures that the rest of the class seemed to be pulling off effortlessly. Even the old guy with the pot belly could reach his toes more easily than Kate could. And standing on one foot? Forget about it. *Tree pose. Ha. I guess I just wasn't cut out to be a tree*, she groused as she toppled over yet again.

Sweat sluiced down her back, her tee-shirt sticking damply between her shoulder blades. That was another thing—the clothes. She was apparently the only person in the room not wearing a skin-tight, yoga-specific outfit from lululemon. *Nobody needs to see my ginormous mammaries in a tank top. No way, no how.* Chances are her boobs would fall right out of a tank top if she did downward dog anyway. It was bad enough that her breasts basically laid on her chin during the inverted-vee posture. *How in the world do women with big boobs do this?* Hers kept seeming to get in the way, no matter how she pretzeled herself. Mercifully, the light sound of a gong indicated that the class was drawing to a close. Obediently, the class followed JP's lead in prostrating themselves on the floor.

"Palms up, eyes closed, feet shoulder-width apart and

relaxed," his mellow voice drifted out in a soothing wave. *Corpse pose, now here's one I can relate to*, Kate smirked. It felt good to just lie there and relax after all that exertion. Before today, she'd always scoffed when anyone told her that yoga was hard work. "Just as hard as any other sport," they said. Now she believed them. Yoga was *work*, and in Kate's book, work was a four-letter word lately. *What I need is more fun, not more work. I'd rather spend my time doing something I enjoy. Taking pictures maybe, or even playing a game of Scrabble. This yoga stuff—it's for the birds.*

The muted lights in the studio brightened as JP adjusted the dimmer switch. One by one, the students stood up and gathered their things to leave. Several of the girls paused to offer some cheerful comment to JP on the way out; more than one flirted outright with him.

Well, I can put a stop to that. Kate strolled over casually, slipping an arm around JP's waist as he chatted with a ponytailed brunette. JP turned to her and planted a quick kiss on her forehead. "Hey, babe," he smiled, then turned and merged right back into his conversation with the brunette. But Kate didn't miss the way the girl's eyes narrowed and she pursed her lips, looking Kate up and down in appraisal. Kate felt a wave of cool jealousy aimed in her direction. She couldn't help but feel a tinge of secret glee. It was an unaccustomed ego-boost to be the girlfriend of such an attractive man.

At last, the room emptied and the scattered blankets and yoga blocks were all put away. As Kate made her way to the door, JP tapped her shoulder.

"And just where do you think you're going?" he asked, his voice low and sexy. She turned to find him eyeing her with that unmistakable Marvin Gaye "Let's Get It On" look.

She gasped. "What, here?" She knew she ought to be excited, but the truth of the matter was that she was rather revolted. The thought of gettin' busy in a room where people sweated for a living dialed her sex-o-meter all the way down to zero. She shuddered. *Ugh, the germs!*

JP was oblivious to her less-than-thrilled body

language. "Yes, here," he nodded eagerly, locking the studio door and dimming the lights once more. He drew Kate securely into his embrace and kissed her until she was breathless.

"JP!" she protested, breaking away for a gasp of air. "If you're trying to influence my opinion of yoga...well, you're doing a pretty darned good job," she joked, trying to lighten the mood. "But this really isn't me. How about we head home, where we can grab a shower instead, and where there's a clean and comfortable bed just waiting for two." She poked out her lower lip and gave him her best cute-pout.

JP seemed caught off guard. His face fell and he released her, stepping away. "Sure. Yeah, whatever. Let's go." He hastily exited the room, not waiting for Kate to catch up.

25 ~ Keepin' It Kate: "Modogamous"

~November 7~

Earlier this year, Roomie said she was giving up on men and becoming modogamous—in other words, monogamous with a dog. I'm beginning to think she may be on to something.

It's taken me a while to get used to having a dog around, but in that time, I've figured one thing out: dogs are a lot simpler to deal with than men. Sure, there are some unpleasant aspects of having a dog, but you know exactly what you're getting into up front: peed-on carpet, doggie-doo, bad breath, and so on. With a man, though, you never know what kind of landmines you're in for. Could be psycho ex-girlfriends, arrest warrants, bad credit—who knows!

But seriously, think about it.

A dog is a cheaper date than a boyfriend, at least in my case. If I take Dog out for a walk, that's free. If I go out with Boyfriend, most of the time I'm the one who pays. And it's not because I make a ton of money, either—Boyfriend just happens to make way less than I do.

(Y'know, I don't need a guy who makes six figures a year, but it'd be nice not to have to worry about supporting Boyfriend financially in the unlikely event that we actually get serious.)

And does Dog get sulky if I'm running late? No. He gets *even more excited* to see me. So excited that he runs to meet me, jumps on me, and covers me with kisses. And sometimes even pees on the floor. (Okay, that's a minus for the dog.) Boyfriend, not so much. **insert petulant Boyfriend face here when I'm even two minutes late**

Dog is delighted to watch whatever I want to watch on TV. All he cares about is snuggling up next to me. The Packers are on? Who cares. Another rerun of *Die Hard: With a Vengeance*? Dog doesn't even notice. *Drop Dead Diva*? Yes, thank you! But Boyfriend? I may as well not even be in the room if there's an episode of *The Walking Dead* on.

Dog doesn't nag me to get out and exercise. Okay, strike that, Dog does beg to go for walks, but that's because *he* wants to exercise, not because he thinks *I* should exercise. And Dog never gives me that judgey-judgey look if I eat a bowl of ice cream, either. Meanwhile, every time Boyfriend goes out for a morning jog, I get that passive-aggressive, "Don't you want to come, too, honey?" Nope. I hate running. Hate it. (If you had a boingy-boingy chest like mine, you'd hate it, too.)

Dog doesn't get pissy when I've had a drink or two too many. Did you ever hear a dog ask, "Do you really need another drink?" No. And by the way, that may be the most annoying statement ever uttered. Nobody *needs* another drink (unless maybe they're having emergency surgery in the Australian Outback with no anesthetic), but if I want another drink, by God, I'm going to have it.

And last but not least, you can train a dog, but you can't train a boyfriend. You'll never win the toilet seat argument, trust me.

26 ~ Canine Kaffeeklatsch

~ November 19 ~

"There's nothing better than a nice, brisk jog on a cold morning, is there, Buster?" JP bent down to scratch the eager husky under its belly. He straightened back up to lock the deadbolt on the front door of the house, then tucked the key away in the zippered pocket on the sleeve of his windbreaker.

"Let's go, boy!" In no time at all, they were halfway down the street to the park. It was 5:45 a.m. *Plenty of time for a run and a coffee before heading off to work.* JP picked up the pace, and the wound-up husky easily matched his stride.

Two miles later, they came to a breathless halt at the barista cart at the far end of Raymond Park. A line had started to form, so he joined in the queue as he caught his breath. He squatted down to tussle Buster's fur affectionately, scratching him behind the ears and lavishing praise on him. "That's a good boy!" he praised his companion, laughing as the happy, panting dog licked his hands.

The sharp clack of shoes approaching caught JP's attention. He glanced behind him to see a petite pair of patent leather pumps come to a halt about a foot away. A quick glance revealed a pair of firm calves sheathed in silken stockings and the flounced hem of a black pin-up-girl skirt. He thought he glimpsed a white petticoat under those ruffles. The image instantly stirred wicked ideas in his mind. He pushed them away with a slight shake of his head and stood up again, glancing back at the newcomer and the handsome canine who sat obediently behind her on a leash.

She was petite, all right. At least a foot shorter than he was. But what a stunner! Even beneath her beige peacoat (sharply detailed, faux fur-lined), he could see that she was a tightly put-together package. Platinum blonde hair was set off by a Burberry scarf, flawless makeup, and succulent lips. He paused for a second to consider those lips, glistening with glossy perfection, and wondered what it would be like to kiss her. The young woman's buckskin gloves no doubt encased pristinely manicured nails, probably in some shade of red. Ruby red, he guessed, and glittery. She definitely looked like a glitter kind of girl. "Hi," he said simply, and smiled.

She smiled back at him. "Hi, yourself." Silence persisted for a moment, as if neither knew what to say next. It was she who broke the ice. "Is this your gorgeous dog?" The dogs were already busy introducing themselves via sniff-test.

"Yes, indeed. Buster," he scratched the dog on the head to get his attention. "Buster, meet...I'm sorry, what's your name?"

She smiled a bit shyly. "Darcy."

"A pleasure to meet you. Buster, meet Darcy. Darcy, meet Buster. And I'm John," he said, forgoing his high school nickname, as he usually did when meeting new people now.

She grinned as she took off one glove (*Yep, bright red nails*, he noted) and offered the husky her hand to sniff before patting his head warmly. "He's beautiful. How old? Looks pretty young to me. A year, maybe?"

"That's about right," said JP, impressed.

"We had a husky when I was a kid," she explained.

"This is my first one, and I can't imagine having any

other breed now. He's so friendly, and easy to take care of, too. So long as he gets enough attention and exercise, that is. But I've got three roommates and a big, fenced-in backyard, so he gets plenty of both." He paid for his coffee and took the steaming cup from the barista, stepping aside so Darcy could place her order.

"And who is this handsome guy?" JP asked, gesturing to an impeccably behaved labrador retriever calmly sitting next to her owner. The dog cocked an eyebrow at him as if in objection to being called "guy."

"Oh, this is Sassafras. She's been in the family for about eight years now."

JP leaned down to the dog. "Nice to meet you too, Sassafras. Or should I say Sassy?" he grinned.

Darcy smiled. "My dad calls her that sometimes. It's rather ironic, since she's just about the quietest dog you'll ever meet. Hardly an ounce of sass to her."

"Sassy it is, then." He looked around at the sky for a minute to gauge the light, then glanced at his watch. "Hey, want to grab a seat for a bit? I've got some time before I have to head to work."

"Sure, why not?" Coffee in hand, Darcy tilted her head in suggestion toward a nearby bench, where they settled in with the dogs. Darcy tucked her coat carefully under her legs as a barrier against the chilled wooden slats. JP welcomed the cold, still heated up from his run.

"So I've never seen you and Buster here before, and we're here a lot," she said, stroking Sassy on the head and sipping her scalding brew. "Are you new to the area?"

"No, I've lived in this neighborhood for years, actually. Buster and I usually come around this time to get our morning jog in. I live a little ways from here, on Whittier Street."

"Really? I'm just off Gibson and Gardner. We're neighbors," she looked pleased. "I usually bring Sassafras here after work. I guess that's why we haven't run into each other before."

"I guess so. Do you work near here?"

"I don't really have a 'job' job. I'm an artist. Mostly painting and sculpture, but I also do some mixed-media work and prints. I got a new printing press about two months ago and I've been learning how to make some pretty cool-looking stuff with it. I don't make a ton of money, but I get by. I love what I do."

"Me, too! I teach yoga, and I work with kids at the Guys and Gals Club. Mostly I work with teens, in the Mentoring Program. A lot of kids out there just need a little help, you know? I love both of my jobs, although neither one pays all that much," he admitted ruefully.

"Money isn't everything." She offered him a smile of encouragement.

Her smile was breathtaking. JP caught himself wondering what it would be like to kiss this lovely creature. "So, where do you do this art thing, anyway?" he asked.

"I rent a little studio not far from here, in Vernon Village. It's in an old brick school building that the city made over into studio workspaces. Down the street from where most of the galleries are."

"Anywhere near The Working Man, by chance?"

"You mean that diner on the corner of Asbury and Elm? It's about three blocks to the west, just across from the Carborough Carryout. You know, the place that sells greasy pepperoni rolls for lunch?"

"Ha! Yeah, I know the place. You can smell the reek of garlic a mile away."

Darcy laughed merrily. "So what about The Working Man? Do you hang out there?"

"It's the family biz. My aunt Rose runs the place now, but it used to be my great uncle Frank's. I worked there all through high school."

"You're kidding! I've been by there a million times, but I've never been in. I guess I don't eat out much. I prefer to cook at home."

"You'll have to come by sometime, and I'll treat you to lunch."

"Sounds good to me," she said. "I'm always down for a free meal. If you're really interested, my next Open House is this Saturday from 12 to 6. We could grab a bite to eat and then you could swing by and check out the studio."

"Perfect. It's a date then." She blushed, and he realized his error. "I mean, not a date, but...oh, you know what I mean. Yeah, I think my girlfriend would get a little pissed if she found out I was making dates with another girl."

"No worries," she held up one hand to wave the blunder aside. "I promise I'll be on my best behavior so you won't get into trouble. Too bad, though..." she said coyly as she finished off her coffee and stood up from the bench to stretch. "I could use a new guy to flirt with."

JP laughed out loud as he got up. "Dang, just my luck. Prettiest girl I've met all week, and I can't even flirt." He winked outrageously. She just smiled, slowly shaking her head back and forth.

"Probably for the best. You seem like trouble."

"You have no idea," he chuckled. Then, his mood shifted as he took a look around the park. The day had fully dawned, morning duskiness giving way to white-bright skies. The air was filled with the sounds of impatient car horns and city bus drivers stomping on rusty breaks. JP sighed and readied Buster for the jog back to their house. "Guess it's time to get going. Reality calls. Until Saturday, then?"

"Sure. I'll meet you at The Working Man at 10:30." She waved a gloved hand and started off toward the park gates.

JP watched her go until she disappeared from sight.

27 ~ Good Darcy / Bad Darcy

~ November 24 ~

The bell jangled, signaling another customer had come through the plain glass door that fronted The Working Man. JP spotted her right away from the counter, where he'd been nursing a cup of coffee and waiting for her arrival. She wore a bright pink vinyl overcoat that fell just below her hipline, cinch-waisted with a black belt. Lime green opaque tights and white go-go boots up to her knees completed the outfit. *She certainly stands out from the crowd in this joint*, he observed to himself, wondering what she had on underneath the coat. *Whatever it is, it certainly can't be too long...*

"Darcy!" he called.

She followed the sound of his voice and nodded with a smile of recognition. Her glossy white boots thumped across the linoleum floor as she made her way over and took a seat. She shrugged her coat off, revealing a swirled mini-dress in neon colors that looked straight out of the '70s.

"Whoa, you look dynamite! Maybe a little overdressed for brunch at our humble diner," he kidded.

She rolled her eyes good-naturedly. "Don't flatter yourself that I'm all dressed up for you. I try to look presentable for the Open House, just in case some actual buyers come through. One of the perks of being an artist is that nobody blinks twice if you dress a little on the wild side."

His mouth quirked into a smile. "Fair enough. Hungry?"

"Starving. Where's the menu?"

*　　*　　*　　*　　*

A deafening clatter of dishes arose from the kitchen. Erma flinched as she slid two slices of homemade pie over the countertop toward JP and Darcy. "Refills?" she waved a metal carafe before them, quickly topping up their mugs. "Thanks, Erma!" JP called after her as she tromped away to investigate the latest disaster in the kitchen. No doubt the notoriously clumsy Ernesto was on duty back there.

"That was the best Dagwood I've had in years," Darcy sighed contentedly and leaned back, patting her distended belly in satisfaction. "I've totally got a food baby in there now," she giggled.

"You really put that sandwich away," JP shook his head, somewhat in disbelief. Even he couldn't finish the Dagwood most of the time. There was at least a pound of meat in there—roast beef, turkey, ham—plus about eight slices of cheddar jack and smoked provolone, vegetables, mayo, pickles, with no less than four slices of grilled Texas toast holding the layers together like a heart-attack torte. Forget the toothpicks; it took twelve-inch wooden skewers to keep this monstrosity from toppling over. Darcy had even eaten the six olives that topped the skewers. Most people tossed those to the side of the plate as mere decoration. And the heap of steak fries? Drowned in tart vinegar, spritzed with a twist of black pepper, and demolished.

"Oh yeah, I can *eat*," she laughed, smacking her lips with relish. "I guess I've just got a super-high metabolism. But I'm also taking in a ton of calories right now because I'm in training."

"What for?"

"Races. I do training runs four or five days a week, and then usually an event of some kind over the weekend. I did one this morning, actually."

"Like what, 5Ks or 10Ks? I've done a few of those, but it's been awhile. Mostly I just jog with Buster anymore."

"Nah, 5Ks aren't my thing. They go by too fast—hardly worth getting out of bed for. I need to hit at least a half-marathon before I feel like I've even started running. That's what I did this morning. Finished in just under two hours. But most of the runs I do are ultramarathons."

"Ultramarathons?" He was drawing a blank.

"They're like a marathon on crack. The ones I do are usually around fifty miles. Once in a while, I run a hundred-miler just to keep my game up."

JP looked stunned. "Geez, and I thought I was an athlete. A hundred miles? That's crazy! How long does that even take? Doesn't it kill your feet, or your knees, or *something*?"

Her laughter tinkled pleasantly through the diner. "It's not that bad. It takes about 30 hours or so, depending on the course. On a flat course, I can probably finish in 27 or 28 hours, but on hilly terrain, it's more like 34 or 35."

"Hours."

Darcy laughed again, with gusto this time. "Yes, hours. If you think about it, 100 miles in 30 hours is only about three miles an hour. Most people can *walk* three miles in an hour without any trouble. I alternate running with walking, and I take a lot of breaks. There are break stations every five miles or so. You can sit and take a rest, get something to eat, refill your water bottles, that kind of thing. The hardest part is not sleeping, but you learn to push through the tiredness and just keep going. Anyway, I don't do those really long runs very often. Maybe once a year or so. It takes a long time to recover from them."

JP let out a low whistle. "Seriously, I'm impressed." Then a tiger-grin crossed his face. "But I guess that would explain your phenomenal legs."

Darcy cackled in surprise. "Boy, you are direct, aren't you? But thank you, I'll take the compliment. Yes, the running is probably why I have such phenomenal legs.

That, and the yoga."

"Something else we have in common! Now that's an activity where I can hold my own. I'm pretty bendy, if I do say so myself."

"You do yoga? That's something most guys don't do." She glanced up and down his prodigious frame. "I bet you stick out like a sore thumb in class."

"I'm sure I do—I'm the instructor," he admitted with modest pride. "I finished my certification last year and started teaching in January."

"Nice. Bet the girls there loooove you," she teased.

He cracked a smile, lifting another forkful of gooey cherry pie to his lips. "I suppose it's possible. I generally try not to mix business with pleasure, though. As Pop likes to say, never shit where you eat. Pardon my French, of course."

Darcy shook her head, bemused. "Words to live by." The last bite of pecan pie remained on her plate; she scooped it up and popped it into her mouth with a satisfied, "Mmmmm."

They sat in silence for a while, sipping coffee and sizing one another up in the quiet corners of their own minds.

"You know," she said suddenly, "this is the nicest time I've had with anyone in a long while. Great food, great conversation—you're so easy to talk to! It's like I've known you for years."

JP's ears reddened with heat, and a pleased grin spread across his face. Her frankness took him by surprise. "You're really something else," he shook his head in wonder. "Believe me, the pleasure has been all mine. In fact, I hope it's not too long before we get together again. I'd really like to get to know you better."

Darcy flushed with happiness, her eyes twinkling. "Me, too."

That was all the encouragement JP needed. He reached over and lifted her hand from the table, enveloping her small, delicate fingers in his much larger ones. Darcy started. He could read her expression as plain as a book: *"But he's got a girlfriend"* was written all over her face. He watched the emotions warring within her, from excitement to uncertainty, waiting in wolfish anticipation to find out who was going to win: Good Darcy or Bad Darcy. They held each other's gaze for a long, breathless moment, and then her fingers slipped away.

28 ~ Douchebag Confessions

~ December 10 ~

The Den was practically vacant at this time on a Tuesday night. An unwatched hockey game hummed in the background beneath the lilt of fifty-year-old Christmas tunes on the jukebox. The bartender dried glasses behind the bar, inventing tasks to keep busy until it was time to clock out. An old blue-hair in a hideous reindeer sweater amused herself at the end of the bar on a touchscreen game, slurping the dregs of a two-hour-old cocktail through a red stir-stick straw. And beside Mitch sat JP, pouring out his heart like a schmuck. A few of the other guys from the scrimmage had come along, too, but Mitch couldn't seem to get away from JP. He glanced with longing at the other guys, seated a few bar stools down and laughing boisterously.

Mitch shook his head. *How the hell did I get roped into this, anyway?* He couldn't believe he'd agreed to take JP out for beers, and at Kate's request, no less. *Well, maybe she's right,* he'd thought to himself at the time. *Maybe he's changed since the old days and I just haven't given him a chance to prove himself.* Little did she imagine that their conversation would mostly focus on her.

"Sometimes I'm not sure why Kate and I are together.

Don't get me wrong, she's a great girl, but something about us just doesn't click. Not the physical side, mind you—that's *hot*..."

Mitch suppressed his gag reflex.

"...but sometimes I feel like I'm playing along because that's what I think I'm *supposed* to do, you know? On the other hand, maybe she *is* the right girl for me and I'm just being an idiot, right?"

Right. Mitch kept his lips firmly shut.

"I dunno. I guess I never thought when we first got together that we'd actually become a couple. So I hang in there and keep trying, waiting to see if things change. And then I think I really *am* an idiot, because if there's one thing I know, it's that people don't change. You have to take them the way they come, and if there's something about a person you can't accept, you may as well give it up and save yourselves both a lot of trouble. Does that make any sense?"

"Sure. But what are you saying? Is there something about Kate that bothers you that much?"

"I don't know. I can't really put my finger on it. We're just totally different people. Sometimes I wonder if we're too different. She's pretty uptight, for one thing. I don't think I'm like that, am I?" JP shot Mitch an appealing glance.

"No, JP, you're definitely not uptight. You're more laid back than almost anyone I know."

"Thanks, bro. I try to take things as they come. But Kate's not like that. She gets worked up about the weirdest things, like last week when I threw a few of my clothes into the laundry with her stuff. Geez, you'd've thought the world was about to end. I didn't think it would be a big deal, but evidently it was. She took my clothes out sopping wet and dumped them on my lap."

Mitch chortled. "Yep, that sounds like Kate. She has her own way of doing things, and you don't want to mess with that. You should've seen the study routine she had going during college. Six o'clock, dinner. Six forty-five, shower. Six-fifty, put on her favorite pink robe and fuzzy slippers. Seven o'clock, turn off the ringer and lock the door. And

God forbid anyone break in on her study time after the door was locked." Mitch gave a theatrical shudder. JP grinned.

"That's not all," JP broke in. "You haven't heard about last week. Apparently, it was our two-month anniversary. First of all, give me a break. A two-month anniversary is bullshit. Six months, maybe, but two months? That's just a blip on the radar. I've had longer relationships with my lunch." Mitch couldn't help but laugh.

"I had no idea it would be important to Kate. I guess I should've known, since she made a big deal at the one-month mark, but yeesh, I never thought it would be a thing *every* month. I mean, that just takes some of the specialness out of it, if you ask me." He swigged his beer, waiting for Mitch to prompt him to go on.

"So what happened? About the two-month anniversary thing?"

"Oh, it was ugly. It all started when she sent me a text in the afternoon, asking what time I was coming over for dinner. Well, I didn't get the message because my phone was dead, and I'll be honest, I'd forgotten we made dinner plans, so that part was my fault. Anyway, I went to the gym after work like I always do, and I stayed later than usual so I could spot a friend on the heavy weights. I ended up getting to her place around 8:00 or so, and she was fuming. There was a cold dinner on the table, candles burned down to stubs—you know, the works. And as if that didn't make me feel bad enough, she was dressed to the nines and looked down her nose at me in my sweaty gym clothes. C'mon, I was at the gym! Of course I was sweaty! Now, I totally understand that she might be upset at me for forgetting about a dinner date, but she really blew her stack."

"Kate has been known to fly off the handle on occasion," Mitch conceded.

They sat in silence for a time, thinking about the woman who drove them both crazy at times. Mitch wondered if JP had any idea of his feelings for Kate. *He must have no clue, otherwise how could he tell me all this stuff?*

A question gnawed at his brain. "So really, what are you saying, JP? It sounds like you're not very happy with Kate."

JP gave a long sigh, exhaling his frustration. "I don't know, man, I just don't know. Maybe we're just not a good match."

Mitch was sorely tempted to seize this opportunity to steer JP away from Kate. But he held his tongue. *If JP is what Kate wants, who am I to interfere?* At least, that's what he told himself. But deep in the back of his mind was the fear that he couldn't give voice: that even if Kate were a free agent again, she wouldn't want to be with him.

29 ~ Keepin' It Kate:
"Do I Really Seem That Stressed?"

~ December 20, 2012 ~

Mele Kalikimaka, folks!

Christmas is my favorite time of year. I love the old Bing Crosby tunes, the happy smiles on people's faces, and getting honest-to-God, hand-written Christmas cards in the mail. And what could be better than snuggling up on the couch under a down comforter with your honey, watching those old claymation classics? Rudolph saving the day, Frosty melting away, and Burl Ives singing the whole silly thing. I even love ice skating (and you know how much I hate the cold).

But the one thing I loathe about Christmas is the gift-giving. I'm terrible at picking out presents, and even worse at faking a positive reaction to less-than-stellar gifts. The reindeer socks that are too thin to actually keep your feet warm in winter. The newly released, horrid album from a band you liked for ten minutes about five years ago. The 6,000 calories of cardboard-tasting chocolate wrapped in shiny foil. Ugh. I'd rather people just saved their money— or better yet, brought a bottle of wine to the party instead.

This Christmas, I had the added bonus of Christmas gifts from the new Boyfriend. Needless to say, I was not looking forward to this. The first gift-giving occasion for any couple is always one to be dreaded, at least to me. It's the moment you find out how well your significant other really knows you, and also whether he was really thinking of you when he bought the gift, or whether he was thinking of himself. And on the flip side, it's the first time you have the pleasure of spending weeks racking your brain trying to think of the perfect gift for him, only to realize that you have no idea, really, what he actually likes or wants.

Here's how things went down. Boyfriend arrives last night with large, shiny gift bag in hand. This is good; bigger bag means hope for multiple presents, at least one of which may be something I like. As it turns out, Boyfriend has thoughtfully put together a care package for me that he calls the "Total Relaxation Package." Apparently, he thinks I'm stressed out. (Now, before we get into the gifts here, let me remind you that Boyfriend is a yoga instructor who has a tendency to drag me to his studio whether I will or no.)

Gift #1: A used, unwrapped CD with scratches on the cover. On the front it reads, "Healing Meditations from Tibet." An airbrushed montage of singing bowls, prayer beads, and orange-robed monks seated in Lotus position hint of instant relaxation to whomever should next press Play.
My reaction: "Wow. That's really...something!"
His thoughts: "I love this CD, and she will, too!"
My thoughts: "I don't meditate."
The gift is really for: Me. I happen to know it's from his personal collection and was given to him by one of his most-idolized instructors at a meditation workshop he went to, so I know he prizes this CD and thinks it is a wonderful gift. And I suppose it wouldn't kill me to give the whole meditation thing a shot. **sigh** Boyfriend gets credit for trying, but I'm afraid I don't love it.

Gifts #2 and #3: White yoga pants and a buttercup-yellow tank top that looks about two sizes too small. The price tag is still on the tank top, covered in several orange layers of "CLEARANCE" stickers.

My reaction: "Gosh, these pants are so soft." Hey, it was the only nice thing I could think of on the spur of the moment.

His thoughts: "She'll look hot in that outfit," and "She can wear them to the studio!"

My thoughts (tank top): "Jiminy Christmas, can I even get the girls into that thing? Even if I do, they'll fall right out again."

My thoughts (pants): I don't even want to go there. The horror! The horror!

The gift is really for: Him. Need I explain? Negative points.

Gift #4: A gift certificate for five classes at his yoga studio.

My reaction: "Wow, five more classes! That's so thoughtful of you, honey."

His thoughts: "Yoga! Yoga! Yoga!"

My thoughts: "Shit. Five more classes. Now I guess I *will* have to go back there again."

The gift is really for: Me, I guess. He thinks it will be good for me. Unless maybe he just wants me to be more flexible, in which case this gift is for him.

So let me sum up what we have: an old CD of music I have no interest in, a cheap, slutty outfit that's way too small, and a reminder that I'm not as fit as Boyfriend is and could use a little work in that department. Winning! Well, one thing is for certain. If I do go back to that studio, I won't be going in white yoga pants and a skin-tight yellow tank top.

Pretty bad overall, but I guess it could have been worse. At least he didn't get me a gift certificate for a Brazilian wax and a vajazzling, right?

Oh, and all of this is not to say that my gifts to him went over much better.

There Boyfriend sits, practically falling off the couch with anticipation, jiggling his foot spastically and rubbing his hands together in glee. I hand over the box that I spent nearly thirty minutes lovingly wrapping and decorating with bows, curling ribbon, and miniature ornaments. It is a work of art. He tears it open in one giant rip without even looking at it.

Inside is a light blue, button-down, Calvin Klein shirt; a classic addition to any man's wardrobe that will last for years. It's met with sickly silence and the worst fake smile I've ever seen. He obviously doesn't like it, and is probably already plotting how to "accidentally" destroy it in the washer.

Then he pulls out the bottle of Eros, by Versace. The scent is heavenly, and the blue bottle is adorable, covered with Greek key designs and a bust of the God of Love. I'm thinking, "Eros, the God of Love...what could be more romantic?"

Boyfriend, on the other hand, says, "Eros? What does that mean?" #GiftGivingFail

The one gift that was a certain winner was the $100+ yoga pants I got him from lululemon. (Yeah, I caved.) What can I say, he dropped so many hints about them that I couldn't have missed them even if I were in a coma.

Note: If you have never heard a jock squeal like a little girl, it's rather amusing. I highly recommend it.

30 ~ PEPPERMINTS AND PAPER SANTAS

~ December 21 ~

Kate cradled her overstuffed stomach with both hands. "I won't need to eat for a week!" she wisecracked, exhaling a puff of frosty white as she stepped outside the rustic Village Inn.

Mitch grinned. The "Dickens of a Christmas" holiday dinner at Chester Historical Village never disappointed. Kate and Mitch had been coming for years, ever since they first discovered their mutual love of all things Christmas-kitsch. Tonight's feast was a smorgasbord of comfort food: creamy potato and corn chowder, pork cutlets in gravy, hand-carved turkey, savory stuffing with oysters, glazed carrots, green bean casserole, mincemeat pie, and endless crusty rolls with hunks of real butter. And now it was time to walk off all of that yummy goodness.

Kate tucked a gloved hand into the crook of Mitch's arm, and they set off to explore under the warm glow of the cast iron street lamps. Garlands of fragrant pine, winter berries, and red velvet ribbons framed every window and doorway. White taper candles gleamed from behind each pane of glass, beckoning visitors to discover the delights awaiting within. Actors in Victorian costumes strolled throughout the village, and Christmas carolers sent paeans of the season heavenward in soft voices.

Kate smiled as two bundled-up urchins raced by, feet clacking over the wooden boards as they raced toward the open doors of the barn at the end of the street. Warmth and light spilled forth from inside, along with the aroma of hot chocolate and roasted chestnuts. The boys' parents hurried after them, just as eager to get out of the cold for a few minutes.

Happy couples were a part of the crowd, too. *Everyone probably thinks we're one of them*, Kate realized, looking at the faces of the people passing by. *How different things might be if I hadn't messed it all up.* She imagined Mitch putting his arm around her waist as they strolled, holding her close "for warmth." Snuggling together under a heavy blanket as the horse-drawn carriage jingled around the square. And of course, getting caught beneath the mistletoe at the entrance to the General Store. She could almost feel Mitch's warm lips meet her own, stealing her breath away and melting her heart.

Kate cleared her throat, bringing herself back to reality. *I shouldn't be thinking about Mitch like that. He isn't interested in me in that way. And anyway, I've got JP.* She chewed at her lower lip and tried to turn her mind to JP's good qualities. But somehow, he always seemed to come up short compared to Mitch.

Mitch interrupted her thoughts with a nudge. "It's the General Store." He pointed across the street to the boardwalk on the other side. "Shall we?"

Kate blushed a little, thinking of the mistletoe again. But she knew that wasn't what he meant. Every year, Kate and Mitch bought Christmas ornaments here as their gift to one another. She treasured each one as a symbol of their friendship. Eight ornaments had been exchanged now since they first met in college. This year's would be the ninth.

Mitch opened the door and waited for her to pass through. The mistletoe hanging from the doorframe sighed down at her in disappointment. She breezed past the displays of old-fashioned candies and woolen scarves, wooden toys and hand-dipped candles, and went straight for the Victorian ornaments in the back.

Mitch grinned, catching up to her a few seconds later. "No fair peeking!" he warned. They never showed each other the ornaments they'd picked out until they were already purchased and in hand.

Kate found the one she wanted for Mitch right away. She tucked it away beneath her coat and hurried to the counter to pay for it before he could sneak a peek. "I'll wait for you outside, okay?" she called over to him. He nodded and waved a still-gloved hand. Stepping back out onto the wooden walkway, Kate sucked in a frosty lungful of air, then puffed out a steamy breath. A happy smile spread over her face. No matter how old she got (and no matter how much she disliked the cold), she always loved seeing her breath hanging in the air. It was like magic.

Mitch emerged from the store a few minutes later. "Got it!" he beamed. Without further ceremony, they exchanged paper bags. Mitch went first, eagerly ripping apart his paper bag. Kate had picked out a thick, cardboard cut-out of an Old World Santa Claus: a kindly looking Kris Kringle, dressed in white fur robes and carrying snowy pine boughs and a small sack of toys. Mitch liked the simple ornaments best.

"I love it," he said softly, and leaned over to give her a quick kiss on the cheek. Then he broke into a huge grin. "Now yours!"

Kate tore open the top of her paper sack carefully and then reached inside. Her fingers caught onto a thin wire ribbon, and she pulled the ornament out. She held up the ornate gold cone and turned it about, a look of wonder on her face. "Mitch, it's gorgeous!" The hollow paper cone was embossed with gold swirls and ivory snowflakes. Glittery beaded fruits in red and green clustered along the top edge, interwoven with sparkling gold ribbons and winking beads that caught the light. Mitch had filled the cone with peppermint candies from the penny jar in the store.

He took the cone from her and emptied out its contents into her hand. "Nine peppermints," he said. "One for every year we've been friends." His eyes softened as he gazed at her with some unreadable expression. "Merry Christmas, Kate." Then he popped one of the candies into his mouth with a broad smile.

"Hey! You just ate our freshman year!" she laughed, poking him in the ribs. "I can't believe we've known each other for nearly a decade," she marveled. Looking at the remaining candies in her hand, she knew she wouldn't trade those years of friendship for anything.

"I can't believe it, either," he snarked. "I have no idea how I've been able to put up with you for so long."

"Oh!" she shrieked, punching him in the arm with her free hand. "Ha ha ha, very funny." Then she giggled, and bumped his shoulder with her own. "Merry Christmas, Mitch. Let's get out of here."

"Yes, let's." Linking arms once more, they strolled away in contented silence.

31 ~ Crappy New Year's

~ December 31 ~

Light had not yet begun to filter through the lacy curtains in the shadowy bedroom. The eerie green luminescence of the clock showed that several hours of darkness still remained; dawn came late on these winter days, so far north. Outside the window, the world wore a thick mask of snow, several weeks deep.

Kate lay toasty and snug in her bed, adrift in dreamy slumber. A faint smile played across her face as blissful sensations seeped through her body. She wriggled in unconscious pleasure beneath the soft, jersey-knit sheets. A firm arm crept around her waist, drawing her into a close embrace. "Mmm, Mitch..." she murmured, turning toward the man's warmth.

"Hmm?" a voice mumbled sleepily, not quite penetrating the layers of her dreams. Kate stirred restlessly, but did not awaken. A sigh escaped her lips, and she settled back down into a quiet, dreamless reverie.

But JP lay awake for the rest of the night, knowing what he'd heard.

*   *   *   *   *

Kate wobbled a bit unsteadily on the golden spiked Stuart Weitzmans she'd bought just for the occasion. She rarely wore heels, so she was thankful for the steady arm of her dashing escort. JP looked spectacular in his classic black tuxedo—freshly shaven, smelling absolutely delicious, and alight with the excitement of New Year's Eve. Kate didn't need to look around the crowded club to know that not a man there could match her handsome date. The sea of female heads that turned in their wake as they made their way through the room spoke volumes.

Although Kate wasn't usually one to draw attention to herself, she knew that her red silk Chinese dress was a show-stopper, too. Its elegant lines cinched at the waist, accenting her curvy figure, and its above-the-knee hemline and daring side-slits showed off her long, shapely legs. Gold embroidery flowed across the dress in the shape of a dragon rising, while simple gold trim edged the hem and collar.

Her eyes swept the room. Single red roses in crystal vases adorned each ivory-draped table. Flowing banners in silver and gold fluttered above, and a ten-piece band filled the room with jazzy funk tunes—a big step up from the usual deejay sets the club hosted. The dancing was heating up on the dance floor, and everyone there was dressed to impress. From satin sheaths and black feather boas to silver mini-dresses and flashing gemstones, the looks dazzled.

Then the waves of people temporarily parted, and Kate spied something that left her speechless.

Mitch. In a suit.

He lingered near the entrance of the club, alone and looking somewhat lost. Kate's pulse ticked upward at the unexpected sight of him. JP might look dapper in that perfect, polished way, but it was Mitch who made her heart race. His usually floppy, adorable mess of hair had been coaxed into order, brushed back in loose waves. And although he wasn't wearing a tuxedo, he still looked sharp in his dark grey suit, black dress shirt, and maroon tie.

What's he doing here? Sure, she'd mentioned it to him the week before, but she was nonetheless surprised to see him. Big crowds were definitely not his thing, and his face clearly showed his discomfort with the throng of people jostling around him.

Without warning, Mitch's dark eyes turned in her direction and locked with her own. Kate's breath caught in her throat as his gaze swept up and down her figure in appraisal. For a few unguarded seconds, Kate could've sworn she felt a powerful surge of attraction directed at her. But then just like that, it was gone. The mask descended, and Mitch's face assumed an impassive demeanor that was impossible to read. Maybe she had just been imagining things. Or maybe she was projecting her own feelings—feelings she had been trying to squash unsuccessfully for months now.

Kate let out her breath and gave Mitch a tentative smile from across the room. She wasn't the only one to spot his arrival, however.

"Mitch!" called JP, waving enthusiastically. "Come on, Kate, let's go say hi." He began to move in that direction, taking Kate along for the ride on his arm. There came Evette, too, elbowing her way through the crowd. Mitch smiled broadly as Evette flung her arms around his neck. That was just Evette; she was a physically affectionate girl, and anyone who spent time in her company learned to get used to it.

"You look smashing!" she raved, gripping him by the lapels of his jacket and giving him an admiring glance.

"Thanks! So do you. Both of you," he added, as Kate and JP made it through the sea of people to join them. He nodded in greeting, smiling coolly and accepting a quick handshake from JP.

"Mitch," Kate murmured, still taken aback at his unexpected appearance at the bash. Luckily, Evette had already launched into a stream of chatter, effectively covering Kate's lost composure. Unfortunately, her overenthusiastic roommate did the exact thing Kate was hoping she wouldn't.

"You should join us!" Evette was urging Mitch. "We have a table just over there, and we've still got an empty seat or two. The more, the merrier!"

Oh, no! was Kate's instant reaction. Having both JP and Mitch at the same table? *Awkward!* Although Mitch hadn't said anything to her directly, it was obvious that JP wasn't his favorite person. *At least JP doesn't know the history between us.* He'd never asked, and she'd never volunteered the information. So far as JP knew, she and Mitch were just good friends. She shot a glance over at Mitch to gauge his reaction to Evette's invitation.

"I'd love to," he demurred, catching Kate's glance and holding it as he spoke, "but I'm waiting for my date." He scanned the people pouring into the club at the nearby entrance. "And there she is!"

A striking, petite blonde emerged from the crowd, garbed in a shimmering gown of ivory and gold. Layers of wispy material draped delicately from silk rosettes gathered at the empire-waist, and hundreds of seed pearls decorated the modest bust of the dress. Thin straps of gold skimmed her exposed shoulders and crisscrossed her bare back, holding the gown up weightlessly. Kate's stomach knotted as she caught a glimpse of the warmth that suffused Mitch's face at the lovely woman's appearance.

Evette's mouth dropped open, her eyes goggling. "Holy cow, she's a friggin' angel!" Kate's mouth thinned; she had to agree. It seemed that Mitch had moved on from her, and wowser, had he hit the Beauty Jackpot. *Not that he shouldn't move on*, she reminded herself. *I'm with JP, and Mitch deserves to be happy. If Mitch and I were going to work out, it would've happened by now. We're just friends. Just friends.* She would keep repeating it to herself until she believed it.

* * * * *

Mitch glanced over and spied Kate amidst the horde of overdressed humanity. Her red dress gleamed, its golden dragon sinking its talons into his heart and commanding every ounce of his attention. She was dazzling. Hunger welled up inside of him as he drank in the vision of this beautiful woman who'd been such a thorn in his side these last few months. As if his thoughts had called to her,

Kate's head turned and she looked his way. He swiftly stifled his feelings, hoping he wasn't as easy to read as he feared.

Kate shone like a jewel on JP's arm, and it stung. *Stupid, meatheaded, good-looking jock*, Mitch groused, still not sure what she saw in him—beyond the obvious, which he definitely didn't want to think about. *Where the heck is my date?*

And then there was Evette, charging into the breach with a flying hug as the happy couple descended upon him. Greetings all around, paired with some idle small talk.

"You should join us! We have a table just over there, and we've still got an empty seat or two. The more, the merrier!"

Uh, except in this case. Mitch couldn't think of anything he'd rather do less than play chums with the man who was schtupping the woman he loved. He attempted to deflect Evette's invitation, and with a best timing ever, his date chose the very moment to appear when she was most desperately wanted. His face split into a huge smile of relief.

Mitch couldn't help but notice the girls' stunned looks as his date approached. He smirked for half a second; it felt good to give Kate just a tiny taste of her own medicine. *She's not the only one who can score a gorgeous date for New Year's.* Darcy looked radiant. Despite her small stature, she floated effortlessly through the mob rather than getting lost amongst them. Some serene aura insulated her from the clamor; people gave way before her with the same deference they would for a queen.

Mitch reached out for Darcy's hand and turned to introduce her. "Everyone, this is..."

"Darcy!" JP cut in, delight shining on his face.

Mitch's face drained as he looked from one to the other. "You two know each other?"

Darcy's cheeks were flushed. "Yes, we do," she said simply, too surprised to elaborate. "Hi, John."

"John?" Kate looked at him in confusion, tugging on his arm to regain his attention.

"JP was my high school nickname," he shrugged. "I really don't go by it much anymore, but sometimes people still introduce me that way, so I just let it slide."

"So you've been letting me call you JP for months when you'd rather be called John? Why didn't you ever say anything?" Kate controlled her tone tightly, trying to keep things light, given the public nature of the conversation.

"I don't know, I guess it didn't bother me, that's all."

"Wait," Darcy broke in, clutching Mitch's arm, "*this* is JP? I can't believe it! And you must be Kate," she eyed Kate sharply.

What the hell was that look for? Kate was taken aback.

"I feel like I already know you," Darcy continued to stare Kate down. "Mitch talks about you all the time."

"Does he?" Kate's lips pressed into a firm slash. "That's funny, he hasn't said a thing about having a new girlfriend."

"Girlfriend?" said Evette and JP at the same time. They eyed each other askance. Kate wanted to vomit.

It was Evette who continued. "Have you been holding out on us, Mitch?"

"And you are?" Darcy challenged Evette quietly, sidestepping the question, which she hadn't been prepared for—and which really wasn't any of this woman's business.

Mitch finally recovered enough from his shock to jump back into the melee. "Whoa, everyone, slow down! Let's all get a drink and then we'll do proper introductions, okay?" His head was spinning; he needed a minute to get a grip on the situation. Without waiting for the group's approval, Mitch disappeared toward the bar with Darcy in tow.

*　　*　　*　　*　　*

Despite the loud music thrumming around them, the table seemed unnaturally quiet. Kate, JP, Mitch, Darcy, George, Cecie, and Evette struggled to make conversation.

"So you guys met at the park?" Cecie prompted JP and Darcy. Kate schooled her face into a neutral expression and took a rather large gulp of her cosmopolitan.

"That's right," Darcy replied evenly.

"I was out for a jog with Buster..." JP said.

"...and I had Sassafras out for a morning walk," Darcy completed the thought. "We both got in line for coffee and just started chatting." They exchanged a small, nostalgic smile.

Sounds innocent enough, Kate surmised, *but*... She remembered how their faces had lit up at the sight of one another just a few minutes ago. *He likes her.* Kate wasn't sure if it was jealousy she felt, relief, or if she was just plain pissed off at the idea of him two-timing her.

Mitch studied Kate closely. *She's jealous of Darcy and JP. Damnit!* Her jealousy made him feel...jealous. *Darcy is here with me. If Kate's going to be jealous of Darcy and anyone, it should be me.* Once again, that great hulking ox was stealing his thunder, and it irked him incredibly.

"And how do you and Darcy know each other?" Evette asked Mitch, interrupting his inner tirade.

"Huh? Oh, we go way back. We met at The Where-house. You know, that old warehouse-slash-art gallery, down on Greyson Street?"

"Isn't that a bondage club now?" Cecie blurted out. "Um, not that I'd know anything about that..." George suppressed a grin and coughed into his hand, looking away innocently.

"That's the one," Mitch confirmed.

Darcy filled in the blanks. "We ran into each other this summer at MacDougal's, out of the blue."

Kate's mouth turned down slightly and she crossed her arms over her chest. *MacDougal's?! That old pick-up joint? She must be a real classy girl to be hanging out in a place like that.* Kate stared down at the table, knowing she wasn't being very fair to Darcy, but she couldn't help herself. She peeked over at JP and found him absorbed by Darcy's every word. *Are you kidding me?! She's got both of my men eating out of the palm of her hand!*

The worst part was, Kate still didn't know how serious things were between Mitch and Pretty Princess here. *Not that it's my place to care about that. Mitch isn't my boyfriend, and never was.*

She began to see with clarity all the ways in which she

and Mitch were made for each other. Glancing over at JP, she couldn't muster up half the affection for him that she had for Mitch. When she thought about her future and chasing down the sunset with the love of her life, it wasn't JP she imagined. It was Mitch. She knew that every day she woke up next to JP was a day she was lying to herself, lying to JP, and lying to Mitch.

She saw clearly, too, how she'd been using JP's good looks to prop up her own sagging ego, long battered by one failed relationship after another. The line stretched all the way back to her college boyfriend, Vance, who'd unceremoniously dumped her on their graduation day. "Aww, come on, babe. You didn't think we were a 'forever' thing, did you?" She cringed in pain at the memory, still hearing that voice ringing in her head. *I haven't been very fair to JP; I never really gave him a chance, because my heart belonged to someone else. No wonder he's been off looking for another girl.* Her jealousy evaporated, righteous anger replaced by a hollowness in her chest. *And if Mitch is gone for good, that's my fault, too.* Kate could hardly blame Darcy for stealing a man who had never been hers in the first place.

She reached out to grab her martini glass for a much-needed swig of the strong stuff, but instead, her shaking hand knocked the glass on its side. Icy liquor splashed across the table, peppering Darcy's pristine dress with obscene pink droplets.

"Oh shit!" Kate jumped up from the table, mortified. "I am *so* sorry! Shit! Here, let me take you to the ladies room and help get that out," she pleaded, feeling doubly bad now at her uncharitable thoughts toward the girl. Darcy seemed too stunned to react, but she allowed Kate to lead her away from the uncomfortable group gathered at the table.

"I'll get you another drink, Kate," JP called after the retreating figures. He turned back to the table to find everyone staring at him, gape-mouthed. "What?"

* * * * *

Darcy held the speckled fabric away from her body with one hand and was dragged by the other by this madwoman named Kate. *Mitch's Kate*, she thought numbly. *The one he's been talking about all year.* But she wasn't just Mitch's Kate, she was JP's Kate. The mystery girlfriend that stood between her and the handsomest, most charming man she'd met in a long, long time. Kate, the woman who shared JP's bed and enjoyed JP's kisses—kisses she herself had dreamed of in tortured silence for weeks.

Darcy wanted to despise Kate with every fiber of her being, but couldn't dredge up the resentment to do it. *I'm the fool here. Falling for a guy with a girlfriend is just plain dumb. Mama taught me better than that.* Shame burned on her cheeks, and she fought the urge to head for the door then and there. Meekly, she followed JP's girlfriend into the ladies room and allowed her to blot the dress with paper towels and cold water.

Darcy inspected the folds of the dress. "Looks like it's all out now."

Kate looked visibly relieved. "Thank goodness! It's such a pretty dress. I'm glad I didn't ruin it."

"Don't worry about it. No harm, no foul."

Kate put one hand to the side of her head and massaged her temple, the stress of the moment fading away. "Can I at least get you a drink? I really do feel awful."

"Thanks, but I think I'm going to get back to Mitch now. I've had enough alcohol for a while."

Well that makes one of us, Kate thought grimly as she watched Darcy disappear. All at once, Kate needed to get away from the crush of people. She craved fresh air and space to think. She started to call after Darcy, but then... *Ah, fuck it. Let them come find me if they want to.*

*　　*　　*　　*　　*

It was Evette who eventually came looking for her. "Where've you been? We've been searching everywhere for you. You've been gone for nearly thirty minutes!" she scolded, eyeballing Kate with concern.

I needed to get away from Mitch and Darcy. "I just needed some air."

"Are you okay? Do you need to go home? I can get JP..."

Kate didn't really want to see JP, either. Now that she knew, without a doubt, that JP wasn't the one for her, she couldn't imagine being with him for one minute longer. *But you can't just break up with your boyfriend on New Year's Eve. That makes a shitty night for everyone.*

"I'm fine," she answered, putting on a brave face and leading the way back into the club. She would get through this night, and her friends would be none the wiser at the turmoil going on inside her. Immediately, though, she found herself face to face with Mitch. *Oh, great.*

"Kate, there you are! We were starting to get worried." His eyebrows drew together, and he ran a hand roughly through his hair which, Kate noticed, had somehow become unruly again. A small, tender smile crossed her face; it just wouldn't be Mitch if his hair actually behaved itself.

"We?" Kate looked around, but it was just Mitch and Evette.

Mitch caught her drift instantly. "The others went to look for you around the club."

"Geez, nobody needed to do that. I guess I've been out here longer than I realized."

They returned to the table, hoping to find the rest of their party, but it was empty. Evette spotted Cecie and George dancing, and slipped away to join them.

Leaving Mitch and Kate alone. *Wonderful.*

Kate noticed another cosmo on the table at her seat. JP must have left it there for her. *God bless that man. He does do some things right.* She picked it up and drained the glass in one gulp while Mitch turned around and around, making a show of looking for their missing dates. JP and Darcy were nowhere to be seen.

And then the music slowed down, and there was nowhere left to hide.

Mitch shook his head with a soft laugh as the first notes of "Lady in Red" drifted through the air. "I think they're playing your song," he smiled, taking in her dress with a sweep of his hand. "Shall we?"

Kate's mouth went dry as her eyes locked on his outstretched palm. She could feel her own hand tremble as she placed it in his. She dared a glance up. The look in his deep, brown eyes nearly made her heart stop beating.

The music swelled as Mitch led Kate to the floor, his eyes never leaving hers for a moment. His arms folded around her, and then her head was on his shoulder, and they were dancing. Every step made Kate hyper-aware of his body pressed closely to hers. The scent of his skin filled her senses, bringing her back to the night they'd shared. She found herself drawing him nearer. His hands stroked the curve of her lower back in gentle caresses.

"Kate," he murmured. She drew back to meet his eye, heart hammering in her chest. He gazed at her with unmistakable longing, then pulled her close again, whispering into her ear as they slowly swayed together.

"Kate, you're the most beautiful woman I've ever seen." Her heart stopped.

*   *   *   *   *

Mitch couldn't believe what he'd just said. But he couldn't help himself. The soft lighting, the perfect song, and of course, Kate. Exasperating, irritating, lovable Kate. He leaned back to catch her eyes as the whispered words trailed off his lips. Mitch wanted nothing more than to kiss this vexatious woman in his arms, right here, right now. Adrenaline coursed through his body, and his inhibitions crumbled away. He found his lips slowly moving closer to hers...closer...he could hardly breathe...closer...

A moment later, Mitch found himself ass-first on the dance floor, crushed under the weight of a rather large lady *not* in red. The flustered woman struggled to roll off him, hindered by a turquoise mermaid gown so tight she was nearly busting out at the seams. A scarlet-faced man in a tuxedo leaned over her, looking distraught as he tried to wrestle her up from the floor. Kate watched with a horrified expression on her face; Mitch couldn't be sure if her dismay was because they had nearly kissed, or because she thought he might be crushed to death.

The poor man helped his date up and made sure she was all right. "I'm so sorry," he apologized to Mitch and Kate, assisting Mitch to his feet. "I was trying to dip her, and she slipped." The couple scurried away from the scene of their disgrace, leaving Kate and Mitch gaping at one another. Kate could still feel the warmth on her back where Mitch had been caressing her just moments before. She shivered, suddenly feeling cold and very alone.

A hand touched her shoulder, and Kate jumped. It was Cecie, with George right behind her. "Everything all right, you two? We saw that lummox crash into you."

"Fine, fine," Mitch blustered, dusting himself off and straightening the sleeves of his jacket. He rubbed the back of his neck uncomfortably, looking anywhere except at Kate.

Kate felt his withdrawal immediately. *I must be out of my mind, thinking he was going to kiss me. Look at him, he's totally embarrassed at something that didn't even happen! He can't even look at me.* Her eyes began to water. *Damnit!* She needed to get the hell out of there. "I'm going to go look for JP. He must be wondering where I am."

Oh, no, not this time, she doesn't. Mitch took off, fast on Kate's heels, throwing a quick "Excuse me" to Cecie and George as he hustled away. He chased her across the club, darting in and out of the knotted cliques of people dancing and drinking. But no matter how fast he went, he couldn't catch up to her. He lost sight of her in the dimly lit crowd. *Damnit!* He plowed forward, hoping desperately to catch sight her. *I'm not going to let her get away this time,* he vowed. And that's when he spotted her, frozen in place, staring into the darkness of the Midnight Lounge.

*   *   *   *   *

JP, Mitch, and Evette were nowhere to be found, having gone off to look for Kate, abandoning Darcy to make small talk with Cecie and George. Nice enough people, but she was definitely the odd man out. She'd slipped away as soon as she could.

Darcy ducked into one of the plush alcoves of the Midnight Lounge, an opulent, shadowy room obviously meant for privacy. *This place looks as good as any to hide out.* She settled onto a snug loveseat and eased back into the cushions. She closed her eyes, idly wishing that JP were there beside her.

Every so often, the universe gives you what you ask for. "Hey, beautiful." Her eyes fluttered open to see the man himself settling onto the sofa next to her. The very scent of him made her mind go blank momentarily. She swallowed nervously and pushed herself up straighter in the seat.

"Where's your boyfriend?"

"Mitch? I don't know." She peered out into the club as if trying to spot him. "And he's not my boyfriend. We're just friends."

JP leaned into the back of the loveseat, sliding down to rest his head at Darcy's eye level. He turned his body in her direction, stretching his long legs out in front of her. As always, he looked utterly relaxed.

"Did you find Kate?"

"Nope," he said simply. "But I didn't look very hard, either."

"You didn't?" Darcy twisted the opal pinky ring on her finger around and around, staring at it to avoid having to meet his eye.

"Nope." He reached out and lifted her hand to examine the ring. The tips of his fingers delicately stroked her palm from below. She swallowed, feeling the hairs on her arms prickle at his touch. "Pretty ring." He eased her hand back onto her lap, but continued to stroke her fingers lightly.

"Thanks." She swallowed again, her stomach tied in knots. She knew she ought to withdraw her hand, but she didn't want to. It was New Year's Eve, and she was alone in a cozy corner with the man who had occupied her thoughts for weeks. She shifted subtly closer, crossing her legs toward him. The hem of her dress drifted up, revealing well-shaped calves in sheer stockings. JP's eyes tracked downward, and so did his hand, now caressing her leg. His touch was hypnotic.

"So you didn't look very hard for Kate." Darcy wished she'd gotten that second drink now. She screwed up her courage. "Why not?"

JP inched closer on the loveseat, his knees now touching hers. His hand roamed toward her hip, skimming across the silky fabric of her dress. "Because I didn't want to find her. I wanted to find you."

Her breath caught as JP leaned over and murmured into her ear, "Darcy, I'm crazy about you. I haven't been able to stop thinking about you since the day we met." The smooth skin of his cheek brushed against her own. His warm breath stirred her hair and sent a shiver down her back. His lips lightly touched her cheek once, twice, leaving a trail of kisses from her ear toward her mouth.

And then JP felt her hand on his chest, pushing him away. "JP, I can't." She scooted to a safer distance. "I want to," she admitted in a low voice, "but you have a girlfriend. Whether you want to be with her or not."

JP slid his hand around the back of her neck and massaged the skin lightly with the tips of his fingers. Her stomach did flip-flops. "Kate is a great girl, but we've been a complete mismatch since the go. We have nothing in common. We don't think alike at all. And besides, any idiot can see that she's in love with Mitch."

Darcy jumped. "What makes you say that?"

"Did you see her face when she caught sight of you tonight? She looked so jealous I thought she might turn green," he smiled wryly. JP tried again to draw Darcy back toward him, but her hand remained planted firmly in the middle of his chest.

"One look? That's not much to go on."

"Maybe not. But she also talks in her sleep...and it's not me she's dreaming about."

"Oh!"

"Yeah, oh."

"Well..." she bent toward him to whisper in a conspiratorial tone, "I have a pretty good feeling that Mitch loves Kate, too." Darcy didn't want to break Mitch's confidence, but surely it couldn't hurt to give her "opinion" on the subject.

"I don't doubt it at all." JP didn't look the least put out. In fact, he seemed rather pleased. He eased back and allowed some space to open up between himself and Darcy. "So here's what I'm thinking. If Kate really loves Mitch, and Mitch really loves Kate, we'd actually be doing them a favor by getting out of their way and letting them figure it out."

Darcy tucked her dress back into place, covering her exposed legs. "I don't know. You may be right...I just don't want anyone to get hurt. It doesn't seem right, this."

For the first time since she'd met him, JP's face looked completely serious. "Well, what's right about keeping two people apart who obviously love each other?"

*   *   *   *   *

Kate was dumbfounded. She'd found JP, all right, but not where she'd expected him to be. She peered into the Midnight Lounge from behind the folds of the velvet curtains at the entrance. JP and Darcy were curled up together on a couch, kissing. And not just kissing—KISSING. *Cheese and rice, even whales have to come up for air once in a while!*

Emotions flooded through her in rapid succession: shock, rage, mortification, hurt, and yes, a little bit of relief, too. *Welp, I wanted to break up with him. Be careful what you wish for, I guess.* Kate didn't want a scene, though. Not tonight. The best thing she could do was back away from the room and play dumb for the rest of the evening. She and JP could hash things out tomorrow, behind closed doors. *Maybe I could fake a stomachache and catch a cab home.* She didn't want to be here anymore anyway, between the awkwardness with Mitch on the dance floor and now this. She made up her mind to turn and go.

But she wasn't fast enough.

*   *   *   *   *

Mitch looked over Kate's shoulder and into the

curtained lounge, where JP and Darcy were clearly visible and making out like champs. His mouth fell open. *Wow, you think you know a girl. I knew JP was a slimeball, but I never expected this from Darcy.*

That's when he noticed the stricken look on Kate's face. His heart squeezed painfully. Fury built up inside of him, and he clenched his fists. In a flash of insight, he suddenly understood what made Kate blow her stack when her emotions went into overdrive. He squared his shoulders and stomped directly over to the loveseat where the tawdry scene was playing out. Kate yearned to flee, but her feet were glued to the carpet. She couldn't tear her eyes away, even knowing that she was about to witness a train wreck. She felt someone slip up behind her; without having to look, she knew it was Evette. She reached back and took her hand, squeezing it for dear life.

"Hey, asshole! Get your hands off my date!" The canoodling couple broke apart hastily. Darcy jumped up from the couch, completely flustered.

"Mitch, I..."

He put a hand in front of Darcy's face, never taking his glowering eyes off JP. "Save it."

She plopped back down next to JP, who remained sprawled on the couch, looking completely unfazed by the interruption. He raised one defiant eyebrow, but said nothing.

"I should've known you were going to be trouble!" snarled Mitch, his lips curling back. "How could you do this to Kate?!"

JP shrugged, peering around Mitch and catching sight of Kate hovering near the entrance. "Sorry, Kate," he shouted over the loud music pounding through the air. He turned back to Mitch with a calm air. "Look, Mitch, this isn't about Kate. It's about me and Darcy. Kate was never the right girl for me, and she knows it." He put his arm around Darcy's shoulders and hugged her to him.

Mitch unleashed a guttural roar that made Kate's hair stand on end. "You lying, cheating sack of shit! You don't deserve a girl like Kate!" He swung around to face her, waving his arms like a crazy man. "Did you know that JP here thinks you're too uptight? He told me so himself!"

"Wait, you guys were talking about me?" Now Kate started to feel the stirrings of anger in the pit of her stomach. "When was that?" Mitch stiffened in surprise. Not the reaction he was expecting.

JP finally unfolded himself from the couch, getting up in no hurry. He held a hand out to Darcy and helped her up. "She's all yours, my friend," JP gave a dismissive wave in Kate's direction. "Though if you had any balls, you would've taken her away from me long ago. She obviously has the hots for you. Any idiot could see it."

"I do not!" Kate exploded, just as Mitch's fist connected with JP's rocky jaw.

JP staggered back from the blow, rubbing his face. "Sonofabitch! Lucky for you I'm a lover, not a fighter. I'll be sending you the doctor's bill for that one." Then he turned to confront Kate. "And as for you? Yeah sure, you don't have the hots for Mitch. That's why you spend so much time with him. That's why you talk about him constantly. And—oh, yes—that's why you call out his name in your sleep."

"She does?" Mitch blinked, his fists unclenching as his head pinballed from Kate to JP and back again.

Kate flushed a deep crimson. "How dare you, JP! I never did any such thing!"

"How would you know? You were asleep."

"You do talk in your sleep," Mitch blurted out.

"Wait, how would *you* know?" JP spat at Mitch. It only took him a second to connect the dots. He rounded on Kate.

"Wow, really, Kate? When was it? Before we started dating, or maybe during? Or maybe you guys are still riding the baloney pony, eh?"

Kate gasped. "Oh, don't *even* try to make this about Mitch and me, when you're the one making out with Mitch's girlfriend right here in front of everybody!" She waved her hands wildly at the gawking spectators who had gathered around. "And not that it's any of your business, but it was before your time, and it only happened once."

"Twice," Mitch corrected, looking a little hurt. "And

Darcy's not my girlfriend."

Kate scowled at him. "She's not?"

"I never said she was."

"You never said she wasn't, either!"

"What do you care?! You don't have the hots for me anyway, remember?" Mitch shouted. He put his hands on his hips and twisted his head away, sucking in a breath to calm himself. He exhaled heavily and then continued. "But you know what? JP was right about one thing. I should've taken you away from him long ago. I should've never let him get to you in the first place. I've regretted it every day since. Do you have any idea what it's been like for me these last few months? The night I spent with you was the best night of my life, Kate. For ten seconds—ten seconds!!!—I dared to think I was going to be happy. I dared to think, *She loves me!* But then you pulled the rug right out from under me and left me flat on my ass."

"Hey, *you're* the one who said we should just be friends!" Kate cried in indignation.

"Yeah, after you bolted the next morning! You couldn't get out of there fast enough. And then you wouldn't speak to me at work! What was I supposed to think? I thought you must be freaking out, and that freaked *me* out. I didn't want to lose you as a friend, Kate. I didn't want to lose you," he said more softly, his voice unsteady.

"And then you started dating *this* douchebag," his voice rose again as he jerked a thumb at JP, who raised one eyebrow but otherwise remained expressionless. "Don't you think it killed me, watching you fall for someone else? Watching you jump into *bed* with someone else? I'll tell you how it felt—it hurt like hell! How could you do it, Kate, after the night we spent together? How could you not *know* that I loved you? That I *still* love you! Everyone else seems to know! Evette knows it," he flung his arm in her direction, "and Cecie and George know it," he flailed his hands at them, too. "Darcy knows it. Heck, even JP figured it out!"

Kate looked around the group in dismay, taking in the guilty expression on Evette's face, the unbearable looks of sympathy from Cecie and George, and the crossed-arm,

"Well, duh" attitude in JP's stance. Darcy just nodded earnestly, a pained look of unease on her face.

But Mitch wasn't finished. "Kate, when you and I spent the night together, I was so sure we had something special. But I guess I was just telling myself what I wanted to hear. Maybe if you weren't so damned oblivious, you might have noticed that there was already a guy who loved you—a guy who needed you—instead of running off to hop into bed with someone else."

Kate's face drained of color and her mouth snapped shut. She found it hard to speak; her mouth had suddenly gone dry. She cleared her throat. "Right. Well, thank you for that, Mitch. I'm pretty sure I've never felt so humiliated in my entire life."

Then she regathered her composure, standing up straight and proud. "JP, I'll find my own ride home. We're through, by the way. Darcy, I'd love to say it's been nice meeting you, but it hasn't. And Mitch? You can go fuck yourself. Happy New Year's, everyone." She stormed off, leaving three speechless people in her wake.

32 ~ SHITCANNED

~ January 2 ~

"...I'm very sorry, ma'am, but we can't take returns on dog food unless the bag is unopened." Kate squeezed her temples between her thumb and forefinger, trying to rub away the stress of the morning. The first day back on the job after the holidays was always hell. Everybody wanted to return things, and nobody could seem to be reasonable about it.

Kate glanced over at Bonnie at the next work station, who was evidently engaged with an equally irate customer, based on the frazzled look on her face. "Kill me," Bonnie mouthed across the aisle, pointing her hand to her head in the shape of a pistol. Kate bobbed her head in commiseration. Meanwhile, Mrs. Roger Crabapple from East Cornfield, Nebraska, continued to rant in her ear at roughly the same frequency that sends dogs into fits of howling.

"Yes, ma'am. I understand. I'm very sorry that Fifi won't eat the dog food you purchased from us, but unfortunately I can't refund your money. Would you consider donating the bag to a pet rescue in your local area, perhaps?" Kate winced and held the phone away from her ear as the customer let out a blue streak of expletives. She hit the Mute button and turned to Bonnie, who'd just finished up her own call. Kate pulled the headset away from her ears just an inch, ready to resume the conversation at a moment's notice.

"Holy crap, Bonnie, this lady on the phone is a real piece of work. What a bitch!"

Kate heard the voice on the other end of the line go silent. Her eyes went round, and she quickly slid the headset back into place.

"What did you just say?!" the whiny voice on the other end screeched. "Did you just call me a B-I-T-C-H?!! Oh, HELL no! I want to speak to your supervisor!" Apparently the Mute button hadn't worked.

"Oh, shit!" Kate blurted out before she could stop herself. She slapped her hand over her mouth, nostrils flaring in panic. "Hold please!" She hit the Hold button before the woman could increase her decibel level even further.

"Oh shit, oh shit! Bonnie, she heard me! She wants to speak to a supervisor! What do I do? What do I *do*?!"

"Apologize, you doofus! And give her something free..."

Kate sucked in her cheeks, gnawing on the flesh inside, her hand shaking as she released the Hold button.

Immediately, "BlahBLAHblahBLAH blahBLAHBLAH BLAH blahBLAH blahBLAH blahBLAH!!!!!!!!!!" filled Kate's ear.

"Ma'am, I'm so very sorry," she tried to break in. "I was totally out of line and should never have said that. It's been a very stressful day around here, not that that's any excuse..."

"You're damned right it's no excuse!" Kate listened numbly as the woman's tirade continued, peppered with more f-bombs than a 2 Live Crew album. She sank further and further down in her chair, sucking her lower lip in and out of her mouth like a pacifier, her eyes wide as saucers. Three minutes later, her outraged caller finally finished up and then demanded to speak with Kate's supervisor again.

"Yes, ma'am," Kate could barely squeak out the words. *I'm in deep shit now.* Tears formed at the corners of her eyes, blurring her vision as she leaned forward to hit the

Transfer button. *Click. Buzzzzzzzzzz...* Kate swiped away the tears hastily and did a double-take at her phone. She looked over at Bonnie, shell-shocked.

"Oh hell. I hung up on her. I didn't mean to! I hit the wrong button!"

Bonnie shook her head and grimaced. "Oh, Kate. You'd better talk to Carol Ann and let her know she may be getting a nasty call any minute now."

Kate nodded slowly, her stomach twisted into knots. She walked the length of the hallway as if through a space-time warp; it seemed to take forever to reach her supervisor's office. But it was already too late by the time she got there. Carol Ann was glued to her chair, her face a pasty white. Her mouth hung open in an O of shock which compressed into a grim line the moment she saw Kate. She flicked her hand at Kate to come forward, shut the door, and sit down in three precise, aggravated motions. Then she put the caller on speaker phone.

"Mrs. Crabapple, I have Kate right here, sitting next to me..."

The next fifteen minutes were the most excruciating of Kate's professional life.

33 ~ THE AFTERMATH

~ January 4 ~

Evette glanced down at the caller ID on her phone and picked up right away. "Hey."

"Hey." Awkward silence.

"You doing okay?" she inquired gently, putting her pen down on the kitchen table next to the stack of papers she was grading. She hadn't spoken to Mitch since the unfortunate scene at the New Year's Eve bash.

Mitch let her query go unanswered. "Have you talked to Kate?" he asked quietly. "She won't return my calls or texts."

Evette hesitated. Kate had left strict instructions that she did not want to speak with Mitch "until further notice." "She's all right, if that's what you're asking."

"Good."

"So how are things at the office now?" Evette couldn't resist prying just a little, hoping to get a bit more information about Kate's unexpected departure from The Pup is Up.

"I wouldn't know. I haven't been back since before the holidays. I took some extra time off this year to be with Mom. First Christmas without Dad, you know."

Evette winced. "Right." She paused. "So you haven't

heard, then."

"Heard what?"

Evette rubbed one hand across her face and sighed. "Kate got fired. I don't know exactly what happened, but apparently she was rude to a customer, and the boss fired her on the spot. They gave her thirty minutes to clean out her desk, and then walked her to the door."

"Holy shit."

"Yeah, holy shit."

"Is she there? Can I talk to her?"

Evette figured she might as well come clean. "She doesn't want to talk to you, Mitch. And she's not here, anyway. She went to stay at her parents' place for a while. It's been a rough week. I think she just needed to get away."

"Oh." More silence. "If you speak to her, will you tell her I called?"

"I'll tell her, Mitch." Evette felt horrible. She still nursed the faintest hope that somehow, he and Kate would make it through this disaster. She tried to give him what little encouragement she could, without saying more than she should. "I think she just needs some space. Give her a little time."

*   *   *   *   *

Kate was livid with herself. She'd made too many stupid mistakes in the past year—especially concerning Mitch. *Sleeping with him in the first place, that was probably a mistake. Running out on him the next morning—another stupid mistake. And then dating JP, when I knew all along that he wasn't really what I wanted...mistake, mistake, mistake.*

At least I have Drama. She caught herself mid-thought. *When did that happen, anyway? I don't even like dogs.* She had certainly surprised herself when she'd asked Evette if she could bring him along on her visit to her parents' place. She gazed down at the furry animal curled up next to her on the faded couch. The pug's squishy face snuggled into the crook of her knees, as much of his body pressed against her as caninely possible. A small smile spread across her face, and she reached down to stroke the dog tenderly between the ears as he slept. Drama twitched and let out a sighing yawn of contentment.

She was starting to understand the appeal of dogs. *Dogs are so easy. Scratch their heads, they love you. Feed them, they love you. Take them for a walk in the park, they love you. Scold them, they love you. Pretty much whatever you do, your dog is going to love you.*

So much easier than men.

Deep down, Kate had known that JP didn't love her. And she didn't love him, either. They hadn't been together long enough to develop the kind of deep love that stood the test of time—the kind of love that had seen as many bad days as good ones. Mitch, though, was another story. Him, she loved. She was sure of that now. Kate imagined what it must have been like for him over the last few months, watching her fall for someone else. Someone who wasn't nearly the man that Mitch was. *What an ass I've been. If only I'd just been honest with Mitch in the beginning and told him how I felt. But now things are hopelessly messed up.*

Kate's cell phone buzzed, Cecie's ring tone breaking the stillness of the living room.

"Hey, girl." Kate braced herself for the onslaught of sympathy.

"Hi, hon. I heard what happened at work from Evette. I thought I'd give you a call to see how you're doing."

Kate let out an ironic laugh. "Well, you couldn't have picked a better time. I'm just sitting here kicking myself for all the stupid things I've done in the past year, and getting fired is pretty close to the top of the list."

"Oh, honey. I'm so sorry."

"Thanks. I just feel so stupid. Five years of hard work, gone in fifteen seconds of Me-and-My-Big-Mouth." Kate continued to scratch Drama on the head. His dark eyes popped open, blinking up at her in sleepy contentment. She gathered the dog up in her arms and dragged him onto her lap, cuddling him close to her chest.

"So what now? Are you going to start looking for a new

job?"

"Yeah, I guess so. What choice do I have? At least I've got some money saved up to get me by for a while. And Evette's rent money will certainly help."

"What are you going to look for? Another customer service job?"

Kate thought about the dreams she'd packed away along with her college textbooks as she settled into the unexpected life of a full-time employee and homeowner. "No. Definitely not that. I never really liked the work, and it's certainly not what I want to do with my life."

"Is there anything I can do?"

Kate pondered the idea for a moment. "Actually, there is. Could you ask George to have his brother Damon call me? He's an archaeology guy, so it might be good to kick around a few ideas with him."

"Sure, no problem. I'm sure he'd be happy to help."

Kate rang off after a few minutes of catching up on Cecie's world, namely the post-holiday, back-to-school hangover at Pine Grove Elementary. It hadn't been so bad for Cecie, who served as school secretary, but Evette had been buried in work as classes resumed. Kate shook her head as she hung up. *I don't know how teachers do it.* All that paperwork, early mornings, rowdy children, helicopter parents...not to mention all the money they spent on classroom supplies. *No, thank you.* But at least Cecie and Evette were doing what they loved.

Unlike me. Suddenly, Kate was struck with the urge to write. She gently scooped the snoozing dog off her legs and reached over to grab her laptop from her bag.

34 ~ Keepin' It Kate:
"Hugs and Ice Cream Cones"

~January 4~

I've never believed in making New Year's resolutions. I mean, if you're trying to be a better person or achieve big goals, isn't that something you should think about every day, not just when the New Year rolls around? But if there were ever a year for me to make an exception to the rule, this is the one.

Why? Because I've failed at becoming an adult. It's a lot harder to do than I thought it would be.

Life was easy when I was a kid. The world was my oyster, and no dream was too big. If there was something I wanted to do, Mom and Dad encouraged me to give it a try. A lot of the time, I succeeded. But even when I didn't, there were hugs and ice cream cones to take away the pain.

Well, where the hell are my hugs and ice cream cones now?!?

(Okay, full disclosure: I'm actually at my parents' house, and have been getting plenty of both hugs and ice cream in the last few days. But you know what I mean here.)

If you had told me on the day I graduated college that five years later, I would be sitting on the couch in my parents' house, sniveling over some guy and some dumb desk job that I never wanted in the first place, worried about paying my mortgage and a never-ending stack of bills, I would've laughed in your face. I never thought I'd be so...*old* at this age. I always pictured myself out in the world, going on adventures, discovering new things, meeting new people. Not to mention, meeting the man of my dreams, who can't help but adore me and treat me like a queen, right? In other words, I should be having the time of my life!

Instead, I feel like Life is having me for breakfast. But I can't blame Life for this one. I created this mess, and now I'm going to have to clean it up.

When did I start going with the flow and letting Life make my choices for me, anyway? I've been taking the Path of Least Resistance instead of the Road Less-Traveled. I should've been fighting the current and swimming upstream. But I didn't. So here I am back at Square One. No job. No boyfriend. And no clue what the hell to do next.

I guess I'd better get started on those resolutions.

35 ~ NEW HORIZONS

~ January 20 ~

Mitch rang the doorbell, shifting his feet restlessly as he waited. It had been three weeks with hardly a word from Kate, beyond the too-short replies she'd been sending in response to his texts. *"I'm fine." "No, I'm not angry." "Don't worry about it." "Gotta go. TTYL."* It was maddening. And then this morning, her text asking him to come over to the condo. He'd missed Kate more than he had ever imagined possible.

His stomach dropped into his shoes as the doorknob rattled and twisted. The door swung open. It was Evette, securely bundled up in a charcoal puffer jacket, trimmed with black faux fur around the hood. She had YakTrax strapped over her boots for tramping through the snow, which was piled over a foot deep in most places around the city. Drama raced out the door and jumped up on Mitch's shins, barking in delight at a new person to pester. Mitch smiled in spite of his nerves and squatted down to pet the pint-sized spazz.

"I was just taking Drama for a walk," Evette said meekly, offering a small smile and a sympathetic touch on the arm. Mitch translated in his own mind: *In other words, "I'm getting the hell out of the way."* He couldn't blame her. His last encounter with Kate had been anything but pretty. Evette ushered him inside and then closed the door after herself as she stepped out onto the salt-strewn sidewalk.

Mitch waited in the entryway, stripping off his gloves and knit cap. The living room was a jumble of cardboard boxes, stacks of books, and piles of clothing. "Kate?" he called out. A rustling sound in the hallway made its way toward the living room, and a huge downy comforter appeared around the corner. Kate popped her head out from behind the blanket and caught sight of him.

"Hi, Mitch," she said simply, dumping her fluffy burden on the couch with a huff. Kate looked fantastic, if a bit rumpled from the morning's work. New haircut, a new outfit, and even light makeup brightened her face. If she'd been hiding away nursing a grudge for the last three weeks, he certainly couldn't tell it by her appearance. If anything, she seemed fresh and determined.

"Hi." He gave her a quick hug, which she returned with tenuous enthusiasm. His throat tightened and he swallowed, trying to clear out the lump that was forming. "What's going on here?" he gestured around the room. "Is Evette moving out?"

"No," she shook her head. "I am."

Mitch's mouth dropped open.

"Sit down, Mitch. Can I get you a beer?" He nodded mutely, struck dumb by her pronouncement.

A minute later, she settled in on the couch next to him, handing him a green bottle and twisting the top off a root beer for herself. He looked at her expectantly.

"I'm going to Greece, Mitch."

"*Greece*?" he spluttered. "What? When? How?" A cold feeling twisted into his stomach and spread through his body. His chest felt numb.

"Soon. Within the next few weeks, actually. That's why I texted you; I wanted to tell you in person. And to clear the air." Her nerves jangled, her heart thumping wildly at all the things she was going to have to say.

"What's going on? Is everything okay? You're not losing the condo, are you?" Mitch asked in rapid fire. "If you need money, Kate..."

She put a hand on his arm to stop him. "No, no. It's nothing like that. It's not a money issue. It's a *me* issue." She pulled her hand back, looking away for a minute and taking a slow sip of beer. She turned to face him again, a look of determination on her face. *I've got to get through this.*

"Losing my job was a real shock. I felt like I'd been run over by a mack truck, and I couldn't see straight. That's why I went home for a while. I knew I needed to take a good, hard look at my life, and that my parents would help me see things more clearly. What we figured out was that getting fired might be just the kick in the pants I needed. This could be my big chance—a chance to start over and do things right.

"You know I've never been thrilled to work at The Pup is Up," she continued. "I took the job because I needed the money. But I should've kept looking for another job, doing something I loved, and I never did. I spent way too long in a job I didn't like, and I don't want to make that mistake again. I've got the chance now to do something that I *do* love: I've applied to join a dig in Athens with one of my old professors this summer, and I've been accepted. It's the dig that George's brother is going on, actually." She looked at Mitch intently, hoping for some kind of positive feedback.

Mitch sat quietly with his hands folded in his lap, a bleak twist to his mouth. "But that's this summer. It's only January. Why go now?"

Kate pulled her knees up to her chin and wrapped her arms around them, slumping forward to rest against her thighs. "I'm not sure I can explain it," she apologized. "It just feels like what I need to do—like it's now or never. I'm afraid if I put off going, it may never happen. I've dreamed about this ever since I was a kid, Mitch, and I don't want to waste one more minute in the wrong line of work. Plus, I've got an 'in' now. Professor Jenkins has a ton of contacts in Athens. He can hook me up with a job, a place to stay—all of that. I may just be waiting tables or making beds at some hostel, but I should be able make enough money to get by. I'm planning to take Greek classes in the months before the dig, and hopefully I'll get an internship with the dig's host institution, too. "

"How long will you be gone?" he asked bleakly.

"The plan is to come back in the fall. Evette's volunteered to look after the condo while I'm away. She's even lined up a friend who wants to sublet my room. That's why I'm packing all this stuff up, for storage."

"Wow, Kate." Mitch looked stunned. "It's a lot to take in." There was so much he wanted to say. How it sounded like a great opportunity. How he was happy for her. And more than anything, how much he would miss her. But his jumbled thoughts refused to translate into words.

One thing needed to be said, though. A question that wouldn't be denied. "What about me, Kate? I told you I loved you. Doesn't that mean anything to you?"

Kate looked down at her feet, then spoke in a low voice. "Yes, of course it does. More than you know. I don't know why I haven't been able to say it, but..." she glanced up, half afraid to meet his eyes. She knew if she messed things up this time she'd never be able to undo the damage. She needed to be perfectly clear. She reached out and laced her fingers through his. "...the truth is that I love you, too, Mitch. And not just as friends." Her breath caught in her throat as she waited for his response.

Mitch closed his eyes, wondering if he'd really heard what he thought he'd just heard. A smile broke across his face, and a warm glow expanded in his chest. A feeling of peace settled over him for the first time in months. He opened his eyes and squeezed Kate's hand, raising it to his lips to place a gentle kiss in the center of her palm. She drew close to him and reached out to cup his face tenderly with her other hand. Slowly, softly, he brushed a lingering kiss across her lips. Mitch could have swept her up then and there and hauled her off to the bedroom, but he knew that there was more left to say.

He pulled away. "But you're still leaving."

The corners of Kate's mouth drooped, and she gave a reluctant nod. "I am."

She let out a shuddering breath of regret. "Mitch, I'm so

sorry about the way I've behaved this past year. I should have been more supportive of you—more understanding of what you were going through when your father died. You know, you said something on New Year's Eve that I'll never forget. You said I was oblivious to you and your feelings. Man, that hurt."

"I said a lot of things I shouldn't have said that night. I've been wanting to apologize, but you wouldn't take my calls..."

"Don't apologize. You were right, and I needed to hear it. I should have been paying more attention to the people that mean the most to me. People like you," she reached out to touch his cheek, then pulled her hand away. "I've been selfish—thinking of myself first and not even realizing it. I wanted to have both you and JP, and that wasn't fair to either of you. I hate that I've acted this way." Tears stung her eyes, and she wiped them away hastily. It pained her to state her past mistakes so baldly, but it had to all come out if she was ever going to put it behind her. Mitch took her hand in his and waited for her to go on.

"Something else you said at New Year's was that night we spent together was the best night of your life. It was the best night of my life, too." Mitch's eyes glowed, and he leaned forward to give her a quick, joyful kiss on the lips.

"I was such an idiot after it happened, though," Kate confessed. "I can't tell you how sorry I am. I think I was just afraid that we would screw our whole friendship up, and you were already so wrecked about your dad. The last thing I wanted to do was add more heartache to your plate. I thought we could go back—pretend it never happened. But clearly, that didn't work."

Kate pressed her lips together to moisten them. The hard part wasn't over yet. "I want to be with you more than anything, Mitch. Even more than I want to go to Greece. And if you asked me to give it up, I probably would. But I don't think that would be the right thing to do. Even if I stayed here, I don't know that we would be happy together.

"I've been going over and over this in my mind since New Year's, and I think the reason I can't seem to be happy with anyone else is because I'm not happy with me. I'm not happy with the work I've been doing, and I'm not happy with the choices I've made in my personal life, either. It's been one wrong man after another, and even when it's been the right man," she looked pointedly into his eyes, "I've been making the wrong decisions. I guess the truth is that I've been afraid to get too deeply involved with anyone. And I'm not happy about that either. I've got more guts than that! Or at least, I should. So yeah, I've got a few things to deal with on my own before I'm going to be happy with who I am. Then, I hope, I can be happy with someone else. Does that make any sense?"

Mitch settled an arm over her shoulders and drew her to his side. Her arms went around his waist, and she rested her head against his shoulder. "Kate, I think you're perfect just the way you are." He tilted her head back and kissed her deeply, beginning to erase all the heartache they had caused each other over the course of the previous year. "But if you feel you've got to make some changes, then you should do it. Nine months isn't that long," he stroked her hair and gazed lovingly into her eyes. "I'll come visit. And I'll be here when you get back, too. Waiting for you to come home to me."

Kate wrapped her arms around his neck, tears of happiness brimming in the corners of her eyes. "And I'll come back to you and spend my every waking minute by your side. I do love you, Mitch. You're the best man I ever met."

"I love you, too, Kate. I have for as long as I can remember." They kissed again, already starting to make up for lost time. Mitch skimmed his lips across the hollow of her breastbone, nuzzling her neck enticingly, tasting her skin with a delicate rasp of his tongue. Her head dropped back and a hot breath escaped her mouth, her blood sizzling at his touch.

"So..." he murmured, leaning back and gliding a hand across her knee with a suggestive smile. "Think you can take a break from packing for a while?"

She grinned. "Oh, I suppose I could spare a minute or two..."

EPILOGUE

KEEPIN' IT KATE: "EVERTHING I NEED TO KNOW, I LEARNED FROM MY DOG"

~January 30~

A lot has happened in the last few weeks. I lost my job. I lost my boyfriend. And I found the love of my life. The New Boyfriend and I are finally on the same page, and it's the happiest I've ever been. Both in *and* out of bed. **wink**

I'm headed out on a new adventure, too. Greece!!! I'll be there for nine months or so, studying the language and helping out on an archaeological dig. (Hear that thumping noise? That's the sound of me trying to kickstart my career.) It's not the greatest timing, given my new romance, but I know he'll be here waiting for me when I get back. We've been friends for too long and we've been through too much together to let a little thing like a nine-month separation come between us. And anyway, he's coming to visit me this summer. Yay! Greek adventure with New Boyfriend! I can't wait to tell you all about it...

As I've been packing for the upcoming trip, though, one thing has really surprised me. How much I'm gonna miss that silly mutt of Roomie's. I guess I've come to love the little guy. At first, I thought Roomie was crazy for getting a dog and imagining that a mere animal could fill the same place in the human heart as another person. But now I have to admit that maybe I was wrong. I can't imagine not waking up to his ugly pug mug every day, begging me to go out for a walk in the cold, horrid sludge. (I won't miss *that* a bit in Greece.) And I'm going to miss snuggling up with him on the couch for our classic film fests on the weekends. (He always lets me pick the movies.) Heck, I think I'm going to miss Dog more than I miss my mom, or even Boyfriend. (Sorry, Charlie!)

Dog has really taught me a lot this year. Things I probably should have learned in kindergarten, but never did. (Or maybe I did, and it's just been so long that I've forgotten them all.) Some of the lessons I've learned from Dog are ones I'll carry with me for the rest of my life:

Lesson 1: *A hug may not fix things, but it will always make you feel better.* I've never been much of a cuddler, but boy, is Dog. At first, it was hard to get used to, and I found myself pushing him off the couch or off the bed or wherever it was I was sitting at the time. Then after a while, I gave up on that. It was a battle I couldn't win. I learned to endure the doggie hair all over my cushions, the wet, face-slobbery kisses, and that sweaty-hot feel of Dog draped over my lap because, frankly, I just couldn't get rid of him.

But then at some point, I found I'd not only gotten used to all of that, but I'd come to look forward to it. My day wasn't complete until I got my daily dose of dog-lovin' in the form of being knocked over with joy at the front door after work, and it felt weird to curl up with a good book if Dog wasn't there for me to use as an armrest. I understand now how pets can fill a place in your life where physical affection is missing, and once you get used to touching and being touched every day, you wonder how you ever lived without it.

Lesson 2: *It's important to listen.* I'm a talker. (Duh.) In fact, I've been accused of having diarrhea of the mouth on more than one occasion. I used to think people who talked to their pets were crazy, but now I see that pets play an important role there, too. People talk for two reasons. One, because they have something to get off their chest, or a message they need to deliver. And two, to connect with others in a personal way. I think one of the reasons I talk so much is because I often feel like I'm not being heard, and that maybe if I just keep putting words out there, someone will actually listen to what I have to say.

Having a dog helped me see my own habit of talking too much and never stopping to listen. Somewhere along the line, I started talking to Dog as if he were a person. And you know what? He cocked his silly head to one side and sat there and listened as if I were the most important person in the world. (And maybe to him, I am.) I had his undivided attention whenever I opened my mouth; that's something I've rarely experienced with a person. And even though Dog may not understand what I'm saying and can't really respond in kind, I know he's listening and that he cares. It's made me think about how I communicate with others, and it's helped me see that sometimes I need to close my mouth and be a listener, too, rather than just a talker. I'm still working on that one, but bear with me, folks. I'm trying.

Lesson 3: *Get out and explore.* Somehow, it ended up being me who takes Dog for walks most of the time, even though he's technically Roomie's dog. It used to bug me when I had to get the leash and take Dog out for his morning constitutional. (Okay, I'm still not a fan of the doggie-bag part—who is?) But then I started learning things from our morning walks, too, as I watched Dog discovering his world.

Dog doesn't just walk. He inspects every little thing. He never passes another pup or a person without checking out the action and saying hello. He seems to find the most mundane items captivating. And no matter how far we ramble, he always wants to go further. The lessons I learned from our walks? Get off your butt and out of the house. Get some exercise. Go exploring. Inspect everything. Take a good look around and appreciate the little things. Greet strangers as if they were old friends. And when life has you on a leash? Make the best of it and go where you can. Enjoy yourself in spite of it all.

Yeah, I'm gonna miss that little squirt.

Okay, so maybe being "modogamous" is a silly idea, and maybe a dog can't really take the place of a Significant Other in the human heart. But he can surely share that space, and maybe even keep it warm until the right person comes along.

~ THE END ~

ABOUT THE AUTHOR

Karen E. Martin, M.Ed. is a full-time freelance writer/editor. She has been in the publishing business since 2004, working on books and publications for major and independent publishers, universities, businesses, and private individuals. Prior to entering the field of publishing, Ms. Martin worked as a Senior EFL Fellow (English as a Foreign Language) for the U.S. Department of State in Romania, a Junior EFL Fellow for the U.S. Department of State in Jordan, and a teacher-trainer for the U.S. Peace Corps in Mauritania, Jordan, Romania, and Morocco. Ms. Martin served as a Peace Corps volunteer for two years, teaching English in the Errachidia Province of Morocco.

ABOUT THE ARTIST

Cover art by **Sara E. Adrian, Fine Artist.** Ms. Adrian's work explores mythology, folklore, and modern primitive themes using painting, drawing, and digital illustration. Her inspiration comes from everything from fairy tales and symbolism to stories and experiences that she and others tell regarding travel, festivals, and contemporary tribal cultures. Authors such as Joseph Campbell, Dr. Clarissa Pinkola Estés, Margot Adler, and others that explore myth and culture have been primary influences, as well artists in the Mexican Mural Movement, Die Bruce, Art Deco, and Byzantine iconic painting from the 12th century. Sara Adrian was born in Columbus Ohio, and received her bachelor's degree at Columbus College of Art and Design.

Thank you!

Before you go, I'd like to thank you for purchasing and reading my book. If you've enjoyed reading it, could you please take a few moments to rate it online? Honest reviews really do help authors succeed. Plus, it's nice to hear feedback from readers on what they liked about the book. Suggested sites include Amazon and Goodreads.

Word of mouth is also a powerful thing, so if you liked the book, please tell your friends on Facebook, Twitter, Pinterest, and wherever else you congregate, online and off! ☺

I'd also love to hear from you in person. You can contact me in any of the following ways:

Email: info@karenemartin.com
Twitter: @KarenEMartin1
Facebook: www.facebook.com/KarenMartinAuthor
Blog: www.KarenEMartin.com/blog
Goodreads: www.goodreads.com/KarenEMartin
Pinterest: www.pinterest.com/KarenEMartin1

Many thanks, dear Reader.

~Karen

www.ingramcontent.com/pod-product-compliance
Lightning Source LLC
Chambersburg PA
CBHW021220260626
47172CB00002B/529